# Tied to You

## BIBI PATERSON

## TIED TO YOU

is dedicated to two amazing people;
the purveyors of far too much information.
I always said it would end up in a book one day.

# CONTENTS

# CONTENTS

# PROLOGUE

He stands at the back of the room watching her, his impassive expression belying the intrigue he feels when he is near her. Olivia Walker is nervously fiddling with the auction brochure as she waits for the next lot to come up, and he can sense the desperation rolling off her. Her posture is stooped as if she is carrying the weight of the world on her shoulders. He runs his eyes over her whole body, taking in the messy brown hair that seems to have a life of its own, the face bare of makeup, the large brown eyes that are the same shade as Oreo cookies and seem to show every emotion she feels. Her small frame is clad in clothes that have clearly seen better days. Today her eyes are haunted; the usual warmth that he has seen in their depths is entirely absent.

For months now he has watched her patiently, waiting for the opportunity to present itself. And today is the day. His cock twitches in his pants and he takes a deep, calming breath, reminding himself that there will be none of that with this girl, this woman. Despite her age, she is clearly more innocent than most, and from the research he has done on her he knows that she is definitely not into the lifestyle. He may be attracted to her—shit, from the first day he noticed her, something about her has called to him—but he is thinking about the bigger picture, and that means keeping things purely platonic.

In all his life, he has never felt a need like this. To most people he comes off as a complete control freak, affable and business-like, but cross him and he will be your enemy for life. At heart, he is a family man; his parents and siblings are the only ones, though, who know just how generous, thoughtful and even protective he can be. To anyone looking at the situation, he would appear crazy, stalkerish even, but she calls out to every protective instinct he possesses. Never before has he felt a stirring to take a relationship with a woman beyond sex, and here he is, stepping into the abyss and doing something he knows is completely bizarre and out of character. Just like the wolf-kid in those vampire movies his niece, Kayla, insisted on making him watch...all he wants is to be there for her, be whomever she needs him to be, do anything for her. She is magnetic, pulling him into her gravitational field, and she doesn't even know it.

But what she needs most of all is a friend. Through his observations of her, he has noticed how independent she is and how there is no one in her life taking care of her. She is working three different jobs just to make ends meet and at night she returns to a shitty little flat in the worst part of Stratford, all so that she can support her mother. All he wants to do is wrap his arms around her and tell her everything is going to be okay. And that scares the fucking life out of him; he doesn't do feelings and that shit with anyone other than his family.

So today he is going to make his move, and he is going to have to do it in a way that she thinks she is making the decision in all of this. She will be his, in whatever way she finds acceptable. The auction is about to start, so he steps forward, taking his place off to the side of Olivia.

# CHAPTER ONE

The pace of the auction is fast and furious, as I surreptitiously check out my main competition. The bids start to slow, but we remain engaged in a battle of wills; this is a fight I cannot afford to lose. Charles Ridings made it abundantly clear that my job was on the line if I did not deliver.

I have no idea why this particular 12th-century manuscript is so important to him, but this is the first time since I started working for Charles twelve months ago that money has been no object. When I first applied for the position, the job description was particularly vague, and the only thing that stood out was the need for a background in rare books. Well, that fit me to a tee. I had just spent the last ten years working as a curator of rare books at the London Museum and, well, circumstances meant that I needed the money this new role was offering. It broke my heart to think about leaving my little cubicle and all the colleagues I had made over the last decade, but the opportunity was too important to pass up.

When I was interviewed for the role, which was never given a formal title, I discovered that it was a rather obscure one. The Ridings, it turned out, were an old family dating back to Anglo-Saxon times and, in the ensuing centuries, had accumulated an enormous amount of wealth and status. But it would seem that, in the last hundred years, luck was not on their side, and much of their wealth dwindled as a result of bad investments and sheer stupidity, as Charles told me in a long-winded monologue about his family's less than illustrious past. To maintain their livelihood and to remain in their family ancestral pile, Charles' ancestors began selling off the contents of the family's library. And essentially that is now my role: to track down and buy back those lost titles, all marked up in detail in beautiful script in an old-fashioned leather-bound ledger, making sure that they are authenticated originals. So, in essence, I am a glorified bounty hunter for books.

Which is why I am now standing in the Christie's auction room, battling it out against some guy who seems as intent as I am on winning. For a moment, I think the guy is going to fold, but then he suddenly ups his bid by an amount that makes the room gasp collectively and I am forced to respond in kind. I glance in his direction, and I can see the muscles working in his jaw as he maintains his concentration. Just then, I feel the soft vibration of my phone in my pocket. There is only one reason that my phone would be ringing at a time like this and my stomach drops. The world spins as I try to catch my breath, my vision tunnelling as I attempt to pull out my phone with shaking fingers. I glance at the screen, only to see that the call has been dropped, though the number is one that I instantly recognise. I let out a small sigh, dreading whatever message will be currently filling my voicemail. All it takes is that momentary loss of concentration for the gavel to come down and the auctioneer to declare the other guy the winner.

I feel myself going pale, the blood draining from my face as I stare across at the man standing there with a smug smirk. The next lot is about to start and I see him glance at me before heading out of his nearest exit. Great, I think to myself as I try to push through the crowd. I finally make it into the corridor to see the man walking away with purpose, and I rush to catch up, trying to smooth down my flyaway locks with my hand as nerves take hold of my body.

"Excuse me, sir?" I call out. The man whips his head around and pierces me with a laser-like glance, and for the first time I really take a proper look at the man I am about to plead my case to. The first thing that strikes me is his height; at five-five I am pretty much always towered over, but this guy is well over six foot. His broad shoulders are encased in a beautifully tailored charcoal suit that seems to be moulded to his body, but the messy, just-too-long-for-corporate hair makes me think he would be just as comfortable in a pair of jeans. But what really grabs me are his eyes; the flint grey colour gives his expression a dark, inscrutable countenance that gives little away.

I keep walking towards him as he waits for me to catch up, his eyes roaming across my body. "Excuse me, sir," I repeat, and at the word "sir," a strange expression crosses his face. But as soon as I blink, it is gone, only to be replaced by a completely neutral expression.

"Yes?" His tone is abrupt, and a little harsh, as he runs a hand through his hair.

"S…s…sorry," I stutter. I wring my hands, desperately trying to summon up the courage I need. I am not a confrontational person in the slightest, nor a particularly forward one, so I am completely out of my comfort zone. I have always been one to fade into the background, waiting for opportunities to present themselves rather than grabbing what I want with both hands. I have heard myself described as passive, but my back is against the wall, and it is now time to sink or swim. "Is there any chance you would be willing to sell the manuscript? My employer, well, money is no object, so I can offer you more than what you just paid."

"No," comes the reply. "If you had been paying attention, then perhaps you would have won, but the auction room is no place for amateurs." I pick up a faint Aussie accent, but the delivery is as cold as ice, and I feel like I am five years old, being told off by my mum. Still I get the weirdest feeling that his reluctance is a ploy, that there is something else going on, like there is a joke somewhere in all of this and I am the last one to be let in on it.

"Please," I implore, dignity going straight out the window. "My job is on the line. I need that manuscript…" I trail off, my mind spinning as I try to school my thoughts into a persuasive argument that will let me obtain the document and preserve my job.

"Well, you should have thought of that before you started playing with your phone in the middle of the auction." I feel like I have been slapped. I have never been talked to like this and part of me wants to tell this arrogant arsehole to go fuck himself, but the saner part of me realises that that would get me nowhere. I have too much riding on this to mess it up.

"Please, I'll do whatever it takes." Okay, maybe that wasn't the best thing to say, but I suddenly see a slight shift in his expression as he reaches into his pocket and draws out a small card. He quickly writes something out on it and then hands it across to me. "Meet me at the address on the back at seven tomorrow evening and we'll discuss this further."

With that, he turns on his heel and stalks off before I can say anything more.

I stare down at the stark white card with the name *Alexander Davenport* embossed in dark grey. I turn it over and see '1 Lombard Street' written in bold script. Hmm, the address rings a bell and I guess that it is somewhere in the City.

I take a deep breath before picking up my phone and clicking on the voicemail icon to retrieve the message that is waiting for me. When the voice informs me that they are calling from Ravenscroft care home, my heart starts to pound rapidly, imagining the worst. Well, the news is almost as bad…my payment didn't go through and now they are requesting that I pay it straight away. I close my eyes knowing that there is no way I can pay the bill, and since I have not managed to secure the manuscript, there won't be any more money coming in until next month. I had been banking on my finder's fee from Charles to pay the bill, and now the only way I can see myself getting out of this mess is to persuade Alexander Davenport somehow to sell me the manuscript before Charles returns from his business trip to Singapore. Hopefully, I can persuade the accounts people to give me a couple of extra days to pull the funds together, so for the second time today I take a deep breath and mentally prepare myself to plead my case.

# CHAPTER TWO

I am trembling as I walk into 1 Lombard Street, a restaurant that is located in the heart of the City of London. I have a vague idea of the man with whom I am about to come face-to-face. My go-to reaction when faced with something, or someone, I am unsure about is to do my research. Forewarned is forearmed, as they say, and the Internet is a marvellous invention. It took a few Google searches to narrow down my Alexander Davenport, but when I finally tracked down the website for Davenport Wines, I was able to confirm that the person I had met was the same guy in the picture on the page of company directors.

From his short biography, I learnt that he is thirty-six and originally from Western Australia. His family own a couple of vineyards and export their vintages globally. Interestingly enough, there is very little about his personal life documented online, which I found a little odd. He is clearly wealthy and from a prestigious family, so I would have thought he would have had some sort of presence online, but apart from pictures at the corporate events that his company sponsors, there is nothing. Obviously a man who keeps his private life just that.

I try to smooth down my wind-tousled bob, very much aware that, despite my efforts at dressing to impress, under my camel-coloured trench coat my black wrap dress has seen better days, and my heels are scuffed. Thank heavens I managed to find a pair of stockings with no holes. I am not sure exactly where I need to go, so I make my way over to the hostess and let her know that I am here to see Mr

Davenport.

With a smile, she leads me across to a partially hidden door, informing me that he is waiting for me in the private dining room. I'm not sure what this all means, but when she opens the door and leads me in, announcing my arrival, I can't help but be impressed by my surroundings. Before I can take in much of anything, though, I see Alexander standing expectantly, apparently waiting for me to make my way across to the table. I reach the table and take off my coat, which is swiftly whisked away by the hostess, and Alexander motions me to take a seat. I smile nervously, feeling thoroughly intimidated by the surroundings and the man sitting across from me.

"Thank you for meeting me, Ms Walker." Alexander's voice is smooth but deep, and weirdly, I feel instantly at ease in his company. I have no idea how he knows my name, but I guess he is the kind of guy who is always in control and so, of course, would have found out my name somehow.

"Mr Davenport," I begin, before he interrupts me.

"Alex, please. I always look around for my father when I hear someone say 'Mr Davenport'." Alex smiles at me, and immediately his face is transformed, giving me a glimpse of the man beneath the suit.

"Alex, thank you for seeing me. If we are being informal, then please call me Olivia. As I said yesterday, I need that manuscript."

"Yes, I understand that, Olivia. You have been very insistent about that. I have a proposition for you," Alex says, his voice having returned to the carefully controlled tone he used when I first walked in. Yet again, I get the impression that there is something going on that I am not privy to.

"Okay…" I say, nervously playing with my hair. "I am all ears." My heart is thumping in my chest, but I am desperately trying to appear calm. A proposition, he said. Well, at this point I am plain out of options so have no choice but to hear him out. I have five days before my mother becomes homeless and that is just not something I can allow.

"Before we go into the details, I need you to be aware that what I am about to tell you is private, so I want your assurance that the details will not leave this room." I nod and wait for him to continue. "I have something you want and I am willing to give it to you, but in return I am going to need something from you."

Okay, I feel slightly on edge at the sound of this, but I am not really in any position to argue. "I understand that." My voice is almost a whisper and I am really starting to wish that I was one of those take-charge kind of people.

"A bit of background on me then. I was born and raised in Perth in Western Australia. My family owns several wineries in Western Australia, as well as various investments throughout Australasia. Basically, we are very wealthy." Okay, nothing I didn't know, or guess, already, but I don't want to give away that I have looked into Alex, so I just nod and stay silent, waiting for him to continue.

"For years, my mother and grandmother have been trying to set me up with the various daughters of their friends, and for the most part, I have managed to avoid it. But now there is real pressure with one particular girl, as both families seem to have gone all nineteenth century. They own the vineyard next to ours and bringing them together would have a huge financial impact on both families."

I raise my eyebrows but stay silent, wondering how this all affects me. "The difficulty, though, is that I partake in a, shall we say, alternative lifestyle, and this means that the marriage is not a possibility. Where I come from, well, let's just say this is not something I could keep under wraps, which in turn could cause problems for the family business, and besides, I could never go into a marriage without being honest about who I am. Plus there is some history there..." Alex trails off, looking uncomfortable for the first time.

"And what does this have to do with me?" I ask curiously, my mind already latching on to this mysterious 'lifestyle' and spinning out in a thousand directions.

"Well, if I were already married, then I could avoid having to deal with any of this. At the moment, it is innuendo and whispers, but I am due to go to Perth in a couple of weeks and I know the pressure is going to be piled on me when I get there."

My mind is racing. "I am guessing that when you say 'already married', you mean me?" I can hear the tremble in my voice. Okay, this was the last thing I was expecting.

"You have got it in one," Alex replies, the smirk that he seems to have been holding back sliding into place.

"Oh...so you are suggesting that, for me to get the manuscript, I have to marry you?" I say, and I can't help the disbelief that has seeped into my voice. What the hell? Has my life suddenly turned into a Harlequin romance novel?

"Correct. I know just how much you need this manuscript, Olivia. Your payment to the care home for your mother has just bounced, and you have a grand total of a hundred pounds in your account. Your rent is due next week, and without this manuscript your boss, Charles Ridings, will fire you and then both you and your mother will be homeless," Alex states in a voice completely devoid of emotion.

I feel like I have been punched in the gut. "How the hell do you know my business?" I exclaim, my voice rising as the anger over this violation of privacy comes to the surface.

"I make it my business to know everything about the person I am dealing with," Alex says, remaining completely calm. Touché. Okay, so I did my homework too, but I certainly did not go into this level of scrutiny. How the hell did he access my bank account? How does he know about my mother?

I fight to calm my emotions, and take a deep breath, knowing that I can't let this situation spin out of control because I am too chickenshit to do what needs to be done. "Okay, so you know why I need the manuscript so much," I mutter, knowing that my anger has turned my face red, and I can feel my heart beating rapidly.

Alex continues in his maddeningly calm manner as if my outburst hadn't even occurred. "I am proposing that we get married, which will solve a major headache for me, and in return you will get your manuscript. Plus I will pay for your mother's care and settle your debts."

"Okay, I get the manuscript, but why would you want to pay for my mother's care? And my debts are nothing to do with you," I say quietly, my mind spinning as to why a perfect stranger would want to do this for me.

"Look, I am not a complete arsehole. You would have to commit to being married to me for a year; it would need to be that long to make sure that my parents believe that we married for love…" Alex fidgets in his seat, and I can see that he is not as cool as he is trying to make out he is.

"What do you mean, love?" I ask, seriously quite confused at this statement. Clearly what we are talking about is nothing to do with emotions and everything about a business transaction.

Alex lets out a deep sigh and pushes his hand through his hair in a gesture that I am quickly getting used to. "My parents met when they were seventeen and have been together ever since, sickeningly in love. And all they want for me and my siblings is to find what they have. They may try and match-make the hell out of me, but they mean well and would never try and force a marriage of convenience on any of us, even for money. Which is why they would have to believe that this is real," Alex replies.

"If you have such a great relationship with your parents, then why don't you tell them the truth? I mean, your 'alternative lifestyle' can't be that bad, can it?" I say, doing my best to keep the bitterness out of my mouth. Suddenly something strikes me. "It's not illegal, is it? I mean, please don't tell me you torture small animals or things like that. Or are you gay?"

"No, I am not gay." Alex lets out a loud laugh, a genuine smile stretching across his face and transforming his features. "And it is nothing illegal. It…it is just not something that they would understand. Look, I don't even expect you to get it, and it's not something I feel comfortable sharing with you at this time anyway.

"So for the next year you would be required to live with me." Seeing my look of confusion, as I am certainly not in any position to move to Australia, he clarifies, "I have a house in London, so you can stay there and still be able to visit your mother and carry on your job. I travel a lot for business, so I wouldn't be around that much, meaning you would have the run of the place. And for the year that we are together, I will make sure that you are looked after, your bills are paid and your mother is taken care of."

My face must display my unease at his words. "As my wife, you will be expected to attend certain functions. You will be mixing with people who are, shall we say, quite snobby, so you will be expected to dress and act the part. It is only fair that you are compensated for it. If you are to agree to our arrangement, I will get a prenuptial agreement drawn up and we can go from there," Alex finishes, an expectant look on his face. I can tell from the kind of person that he is that he is probably used to people jumping at his command, agreeing with him instantly, but I need a moment to gather my thoughts.

"So let me get this straight," I say seriously. "If I agree to marry you for one year, then you will let me buy the manuscript and you will pay my expenses during the course of the year?" In my mind's eye I see a giant grandfather clock going tick-tock, tick-tock, a countdown as I consider my future.

"In a nutshell…" Alex trails off as I stare at the tablecloth, my mind whirring with everything Alex has just said.

"Look, Olivia, I know this is a lot to take in, but I think for both of us, time is of the essence. I have ordered us some food, so let's just forget about everything for the moment and enjoy our meal, and then perhaps you can go away and have a think about my proposal," Alex suggests placidly, as if we have been discussing a simple business deal and not friggin' marriage.

Alex gets up and presses a button on the wall. A couple of minutes later a waiter walks in, carrying two plates. As he sets them down in front of us, I can see fillet of beef Wellington, green beans, sautéed potato and creamy mushrooms. My stomach suddenly rumbles and I realise that I am ravenous, especially because I haven't eaten since breakfast. Without asking, Alex pours me a glass of red wine and puts it in front of me.

"Um, thanks, but I don't really drink. I'll just have water if you don't mind," I say, not sure that I want to start going into the reasons why I don't drink. That is a whole can of worms for another day.

Alex gives me a quizzical look but doesn't question me, simply taking away the glass and giving me the choice of still or sparkling water instead. We both dig into our food and the silence is a welcome relief to the conversation that we have just been having. I go through everything Alex has told me and I know realistically that I don't have any other choice; I cannot risk my mother becoming homeless. I would love to scream and wail about how life is so unfair...blah, blah, blah, but the reality is that Alex's offer is actually the light at the end of a really long, dark tunnel and I just can't see any other way out of the current mess that is my life.

As I reflect on the situation, it strikes me a little like that film *Indecent Proposal*, but Alex is certainly way hotter than Robert Redford and I am certainly no Demi Moore. "Do you expect me to have sex with you?" I suddenly blurt out, the filter on my brain failing to kick in before my mouth takes off, as I feel the blush creep across my face.

Alex looks at me with a strangely soft expression. "No, Olivia. That is not part of this deal. Believe me when I say that I think you are far too innocent to deal with what I offer." His statement confuses the hell out of me. Innocent? At thirty-three, I would hardly think that I am some innocent virgin. I have had two long-term relationships, a couple of short, torrid affairs and a series of one-night stands, so no, I don't think so. But I am not about to start discussing my sex life with Alex. I am merely relieved that there are no expectations on his part.

I find myself pushing the remains of my meal around my plate, my stomach suddenly too full for me to take another mouthful. The food was delicious, but I don't feel like I have fully done it justice in my current distracted state. I glance over at Alex, and as ever through this strange meeting, he seems to have remained completely calm—impassive almost. I study him under my lashes and while I certainly am attracted to him—well, what normal girl wouldn't be attracted to a gorgeous hunk with a dreamy accent?— what strikes me most is how calm I feel in his presence. I would have thought I would be a bundle of nerves, but actually, with the sex issue clarified, I feel surprisingly safe, a strange feeling for me as I have essentially been looking after myself since I was twenty.

"Okay, I'll do it," I say softly. Alex looks at me, surprise written across his expression. I don't think he thought I would make a decision so quickly.

He wipes his mouth with the pristine white cloth napkin. "Good. I'll get the papers drawn up and sent across to you first thing." Alex looks me in the eye, almost daring me to retract my acceptance of his proposal, but I look at him steadfastly.

"If you don't mind, I think I am going to head home," I say, knowing that I need to leave before I change my mind. "I think I have a migraine coming and need to take some tablets," I lie smoothly. I think Alex realises my lie when I see a shadow cross his expression, but thankfully he doesn't call me on it. Ever the gentleman, he insists on collecting my coat, helping me into it with a practiced ease, walking me out and putting me in his car, with strict instructions to the driver to deliver me home. I look out the window at Alex standing on the pavement, hands stuffed in his pockets, his expression strangely triumphant, as the car pulls away, and I am instantly swamped with the overwhelming sensation that life is never going to be the same.

The journey home is mercifully quick, the London traffic surprisingly light for a Wednesday evening, and when the car pulls up in front of my building, I scramble for the door handle. When I try to pay for my ride, the driver insists that it is on Mr Davenport's account. I thank him and wish him a good evening before heading inside to begin my night of contemplation over the strange situation I find myself in.

# CHAPTER THREE

I wake to the incessant ringing of my doorbell. I fling on my robe before opening the door to find a courier standing there, holding a stack of packages. "Ms Walker?" he asks. I nod and sign for my parcels before heading back into my flat. My tiny studio is sparse; the escalation of my mother's disease and mounting costs for her care have directly correlated with the slow selling off of my worldly goods and the downsizing of my living arrangements.

I leave the parcels on the table and then head over to the cupboard that houses the little kitchenette area. I pop the kettle on and make myself a cup of tea before sitting down to open the packages. The first box contains a smartphone, all shiny and new compared with the completely basic phone that I own. There is no note attached, but my assumption is that this is from Alex. After all, who else would be sending me things?

I plug the phone in to charge before turning my attention to a large flat box. When I finally pull out the contents, I find myself holding a small laptop and I guess it is one of those Chromebook computers that seem to be all the rage at the moment. Not sure if it needs charging as well, I plug the computer in and then turn my attention to the third and final package. Seconds later and I am holding the manuscript in my hands along with a handwritten note from Alex:

*Dear Olivia,*
*As promised here is your manuscript. I trust that you will still honour our arrangement. We can discuss payment separately.*

*The laptop and phone are encrypted, so please ensure that you use them for all communication between us. You will find my details already stored on both devices, and I have set up a new email account for you.*

*I have emailed you a copy of the prenuptial agreement that I have had drawn up. If you are happy with the terms, you can sign it electronically and email it back.*

*Any questions, just drop me an email.*

*All the best,*

*Alex*

The note is impersonal and business-like, which suits me fine. This is a business arrangement, after all. I sip on my tea as I wait for the laptop to load. When the home screen is finally up, I click on the email icon and then open up the email that is waiting for me.

I read through the attached document, my brain swimming as I try to read between the lines of 'legalese'. As I understand it, the contract states that if we remain married for a full year, Alex will take care of all my debts and my mother's care for the year that we are together and I will get a payout of a million pounds when we divorce. What surprises me most is the caveat about 'extramarital relations'. It appears that I am perfectly fine to have a lover as long as I am discreet. Okay, I hadn't even thought about that. It also states that Alex will also be able to make his visits to his 'club', though I am not sure what that means. Maybe this lifestyle thing is a secret society or something equally obscure. I find myself grinning as my imagination conjures up an image of hooded men exchanging strange handshakes in a darkened room lined with sconces.

I spend some time chewing over the document as

I finish my cup of tea, trying to figure out the source of my unease. It is not the idea of being able to have another relationship whilst being married; I will be fine…it's not like I am not used to being on my own, but a year is a long time for a guy to go without, I guess. No, it is the idea of the payoff at the end. With trembling fingers, I reach for the new phone, find Alex's direct line and hit dial. I am relieved when he answers after a couple of rings.

"Good morning, Olivia," says Alex smoothly. I wonder how the hell he knows it is me, but then I realise he has already programmed his number, so its stands to reason he knows mine.

"Morning, Alex. Are you okay to chat for a couple of minutes? I don't want to interrupt your day," I ask. Inwardly I am cursing the tremble that I hear in my voice, the nerves making themselves apparent.

"Sure thing. I guess you have had a chance to read through the document?" Alex asks, his voice calm and even, as if he is completely unaffected by the deal we are about to strike.

"Yes. And thank you for the phone and laptop, by the way. You didn't need to," I say, still feeling a little weirded out by Alex's generosity. There was no need to have sent over what must be top-of-the-line gadgets; basic models would have certainly done me.

"Actually I did. I need to know that our conversations are secure. I can't risk this kind of information getting out. So what can I help you with?" asks Alex.

"Um, the payoff…the million pounds…I don't want it!" I blurt, anxiety flooding me.

For a moment, there is silence. "You don't want the money?" Alex sounds incredulous.

20

"No, look, I appreciate your helping with my mother's care and looking after me during the year we are married, but there is no need for anything else. Really, I don't want it. It is not something I will have earned." I can hear my voice rising, but I try my best to control my emotions.

"Believe me, you will have earned it by the end of the year," Alex retorts, his voice hard and firm.

"Even so, Alex. I don't feel comfortable with taking that kind of money. Please…I am happy to agree to everything else, but could you take that point out?" I request, and I hate myself when I hear the quaver in my voice. I don't want to beg, but damn it, I will if I have to. This is just not something I will compromise on.

With a sigh, Alex acquiesces and promises me that a new version will be sent out within the hour. When I put the phone down, it immediately rings again, and puzzled by the unknown number showing on the screen along with uncertainty of who would actually have this number, I answer with a cautious "Hello?"

I am beyond surprised when the director of the care facility introduces herself, and my stomach twists into knots as I wait for her to start talking about chucking my mother out. Instead, she starts gushing about the very generous donation that my fiancé has made to the facility. That, combined with the news that my mother has now been moved to a superior room with a view of the garden, already prepaid for the coming year, brings silent tears to my eyes. It would seem that Alex has already been very busy this morning.

When I finally get off the phone, I am able to break down with the relief that my mother is going to be okay. I sob loudly, letting out all the stress and tension that I have been keeping locked up tight. The crying is cathartic, and by the time my tears start to dry up, I finally feel something haven't for a very long time…hope.

# CHAPTER FOUR

The background roar of the plane's engines filters through my dreams. I am lying in my first-class bed with my eyes closed, contemplating the last ten days. In such a short space of time, Alex has turned my world upside down. Once the agreement was signed, he insisted I give notice on my flat, as well as my supplementary jobs, and move into his townhouse in Chelsea. I managed to stall—though in hindsight I really wonder why—so now my meagre possessions are being moved by his housekeeper while I am flying and I feel guilty that someone is being forced to deal with my mess.

My boss, Charles, was delighted with the manuscript, though I never let him know what lengths it took to get it for him. He wouldn't have been interested anyway! Instead, I requested the holiday leave I am entitled to and let him know that I would be coming back from Australia married. I almost laughed at the look of surprise on his face when I told him, but managed to stay cool and professional.

I keep my eyes closed and continue to pretend that I am asleep. I can hear the soft tapping as Alex continues to work on his laptop, something he has done non-stop since we boarded the plane in Singapore. We have barely spoken, beyond the arrangements to get us to Australia, and even then most of that was done through his secretary. I made the first leg of the journey alone as Alex had already flown out to do business in Singapore. I had never flown long distance before and was like a kid in a candy store being in first class, though some of the novelty had worn off by the time that I met Alex in the departure lounge for our second flight.

It is not long before people start moving around more and I realise that we will be coming in to land soon. I crack open my eyes and am startled to find Alex staring directly at me, with an expression that I can't fathom across his face. "Sorry, was I snoring?" I ask, surreptitiously wiping my chin in case any drool escaped.

"No, you are all good," Alex says, letting out a dry laugh. "Sleep well?"

I nod as I stretch my arms above my head. Seriously, I am not sure if I could ever fly economy again if this is what it's like in first class. The aroma of freshly baked rolls wafts through the cabin and my stomach growls embarrassingly. My body clock is all over the place and my stomach doesn't know whether it wants breakfast, lunch or dinner, but at least I have managed to get a decent sleep. I am just hoping that the jet lag is not going to be too bad. I glance at my watch, which I seem to have reset several times already, and it tells me that it is 7 a.m. Okay, that means breakfast. I can deal with that.

I grab my bag and head into a toilet cubicle to freshen up, glad that I brought a change of clothes with me. I wash my face and then slip into a pale yellow sundress, brushing the tangles out of my choppy dark brown bob. I add a final slick of lip gloss and then make my way back to my seat to find my breakfast tray waiting for me. Yum.

"I ordered you a tea. I hope that's okay?" Alex asks, looking at me expectantly.

"Fab, thanks, Alex," I mumble through a bite of

freshly baked croissant. Really, I need to get some manners so that I don't just dive into my food, I think to myself. Alex attacks his breakfast with equal gusto, sipping on a cup of strong coffee. I love the aroma of freshly brewed coffee—just a shame the taste doesn't measure up. I'll stick to my tea, thank you very much.

Once our trays are cleared away, I settle back and stare out the window at the beautiful blue sky. I am nervous and find myself twisting my fingers in agitation. I fiddle with the large diamond currently nestling on my ring finger, unused to its new weight. "Are you okay, Olivia?" Alex asks softly, breaking through my reverie.

I offer a small smile in response. "Just a bit nervous about meeting your family. I don't want to let you down, Alex. I know you have a lot riding on this. I have done my best to memorise all that info you sent across, but I am just worried that I will slip up at some point. I am really just about the world's worst liar."

"Don't worry about it, Olivia. They are going to love you. Look, we have a couple days before the big meet-and-greet, so I will talk to my mum first about stuff, though they know about you already, and you can relax and soak up some sun. We'll work out the details of the ceremony and stuff this week and go from there. You don't have to worry about organising a thing." Alex's tone is soothing, and all at once I feel calmer. I still don't know what super power he seems to possess that instantly makes me feel all Zen-like.

"Okay, thanks, Alex. This is not your everyday kind of situation and I really don't want to mess it up. You have been so good to me, sorting my mother out and everything, and now it's my turn to step up to the plate."

"Stop worrying. Let me take care of everything, okay?" says Alex, his voice and expression firm.

"Okey-dokes," I answer knowing that, despite its futility, I will continue to worry regardless.

We chat a bit further as I probe Alex about our destination. I had never even really heard of Perth before Alex told me that he was born there. Since then, I had bought a Lonely Planet guide and marked up the pages of things I wanted to do and see, but I have no real idea on the distances between stuff. All I really want to do is see a kangaroo…god I am such a child, I think to myself.

Before I know it, the seatbelt sign blinks on, and we start our descent. It is not long before we have landed and been whisked through passport control, and then we are walking through the doors into the arrivals hall. I can see Alex scanning the people waiting and I feel myself getting a lump in my throat as I watch people greeting each other, often with tears in their eyes. Alex clears his throat and indicates towards a tall, well-built guy with a shaved head dressed in a driver's uniform, holding a smart placard stating Davenport. Sliding his hand through mine, Alex murmurs softly, "Remember, you are my blushing bride-to-be." I find myself blushing at his words, and satisfied that I am behaving suitably fiancée-like, we walk across to greet the man.

"Alex," he cries when he notices us.

"All right, Shane?" Alex responds and I notice his accent becoming a little stronger. "Shane, this is Olivia, my fiancée." Alex introduces me, and I shake Shane's proffered hand.

"Hi," I say shyly, feeling instantly intimidated by

the tall guy in front of me. He is tanned and gorgeous with striking blue eyes, everything I would normally be attracted to, but today I feel nothing.

"Well, she's a beaut," Shane says, smirking at me.

"Enough, she's mine. Hands off, dude," says Alex smoothly, before engaging Shane in conversation. From what I can gather, they are old friends and soon they are in a heated discussion about some sports team called the Dockers. Men.

I follow them out of the door and am stunned by the wall of heat I walk into as we step outside. Alex had warned me that Perth was hot in November, but this is like an oven. I am grateful when we finally arrive at the car and I can slide into the air-conditioned coolness. Both men pretty much ignore me as they catch up, which suits me fine, as it gives me a chance to take in the world around me. The landscape is so different from what I am used to, and I kind of feel like it is all a bit surreal. The bush is so brown compared with the green fields of England and I can see the heat shimmering off the tar road. The buildings are completely at odds with what I am used to, but I drink it all in as we get on the highway.

"So how come you guys are staying at the Crown Perth?" Shane asks, breaking me out of my musings.

"Didn't think it would be fair to Olivia to meet the folks the minute she stepped off the plane," Alex responds with a laugh that tells me that Shane must know the family well.

"Nice," Shane says with a smirk.

Minutes later we are pulling up under a canopy at the entrance to the most luxurious hotel I have ever seen. As we drove up to the building, it glowed like a giant white pyramid and I wondered if we had been transported to another planet, the structure so alien compared with everything around it. But now all I can think about is not tripping up and embarrassing myself. As I climb out the car, I am once again assaulted by the hot, arid air. I head around to grab my small case, but before I have a chance, a bellhop is loading all the bags onto a trolley and whisking them away. I squeak in protest, but Alex assures me that they will be taken straight up to the suite. Suite? Like, not just a room?

With a fond farewell to Shane and promise of beers on the beach, Alex takes my arm and steers me to the reception desk. We are swiftly checked in and I can't help but notice the girl blatantly checking Alex out. I have to hide my inward smirk as I place my hand, complete with the giant diamond engagement ring that Alex presented me with on the plane, on his arm and smile sweetly across at her. I feel Alex shaking slightly and I realise he is laughing silently at the scene unfolding. I look up into his grey eyes and see mirth shining out and I give him a genuine smile, probably one of my first since this whole thing started, in return. The receptionist takes this all in and I can see a faint blush under her makeup; she has obviously got the message. Ours may be a marriage of convenience, but if I am playing the role of a blushing bride, I am not going to have some random girl undermining our façade.

The receptionist, whose name tag reads Janie, hands over the key cards and then wishes us a pleasant stay. Alex puts an arm around me and guides me back towards the lifts, murmuring into my ear, "Well played, Olivia." I smile and shiver slightly, despite the heat radiating off Alex's solid frame.

"You can call me Liv if you want. That's what my friends call me," I murmur back.

"Liv. Hmm, I like it. Suits you." Alex responds, his hot breath in my ear making my knees feel weak. I sternly remind myself that this is an act, this is not real, and this is not about romance or even sex. At last we reach the suite, and when Alex opens the door, I actually gasp as I take in my surroundings. The décor is plush and modern, but what really grabs me when we walk into the living area is the stunning view of the city across the river beyond the windows.

"You take the master," Alex instructs, and when I go to refuse the look that he gives me brooks no argument.

"Wow, Alex, seriously, this is amazing. That view…" I trail off.

"Yeah, it is pretty awesome. That's why I chose the suite. Can't get much better than that," Alex says softly. I am guessing that this view is familiar to him as he seems to know his way around the suite, but even so, he seems as enamoured by it as I am. I see the doors leading onto the balcony and step out, despite the heat, to get a better look.

I am not sure how long I stand there taking in the sights and smells, but I am startled back to reality when Alex walks through the doors in long board shorts and a T-shirt, his hair still damp from the shower he must have just had. "You should put some cream on," Alex states. "You'll burn to a crisp otherwise." I glance down at my shoulders and see that my normally milky-white skin is already turning pink.

"Definitely, the last thing I want is to get sunburnt first day here." I laugh. I head back indoors and make my way through to my room. Really, this is all too much. I am not used to this kind of luxury and it kind of freaks me out a bit. But as I eye the bed I can't help but fling myself down onto it, enjoying the crispness of the sheets against my overheated skin. Despite the sleep I managed to get on the plane, it is only moments before I find myself dozing off.

*~*~*~*

"Wake up, sleepyhead." Strong fingers grip my shoulder gently and I feel myself being shaken from my deep slumber. I mumble, wondering who the hell is waking me up, as I roll over onto my back. I crack open my eyes to find Alex staring back at me, and it feels a little like déjà vu as he looks at me with that same expression he had on the plane.

"Argh, what time is it?" I ask, running a hand through my hair.

"Just after one. Thought you might be hungry." Alex responds, just as my stomach lets out a grumble, making us both laugh.

"You thought right," I say. "Yeah, food would be good."

"Come on. I thought we could eat down at the grill by the pool. There should be a bit of a breeze and you won't catch too much sun." I glance down at my shoulders and can see the smattering of freckles coming through where the sun caught me earlier.

We make our way down through the hotel and find a free table at the grill. I watch the people splashing around in the water and make a note to dig out my costume later and come back for a swim; the water looks sublime. The service is brisk and in no time at all I am sipping on a wonderfully cool mango smoothie whilst Alex drinks a bottle of beer. We chat softly as Alex fills me in a little about the history of Perth while we wait for our food. When it arrives I dig into my club sandwich with delight.

"I love watching you eat," Alex says suddenly, and all at once I feel very self-conscious. I feel my face go red and I have no idea what he means by that. "What I mean," he clarifies, seeing my confusion, "is that you enjoy your food. So many women just order food and then push it around the plate, barely tasting anything. Yet you eat each mouthful like it is the best thing you have ever tasted. Like you might never get to eat it again."

I can feel my cheeks glowing with my shame, but I realise I have nothing to lose by telling the truth. "That's because this food is divine compared to what I normally eat. And usually, I don't know when I am going to eat next." My words are soft and I can see Alex doesn't really understand. "Every penny I made went towards my mother's care and sometimes there just wasn't enough for me. So sometimes I survived on bread and soup and noodles." I can't meet Alex's eyes, so I stare at the floor fixedly instead. "And sometimes there wasn't even enough for that, so I would have to sell something just so I could pay the rent and there wouldn't be enough for food at all."

A finger hooks under my chin, forcing me to look up into Alex's stormy grey eyes. There is no pity, just compassion, and I feel Alex's thumb stroke my cheek. "It's going to be okay, Liv," Alex promises. "You will never go back to that, okay?" I just nod, not really knowing what else to say, while I blink away the tears forming in my eyes. I am definitely not telling him that I am already saving for when I have to leave in a year's time so that I don't have to experience the ache of a hungry belly again.

"Right, what do you want to do this afternoon?" Alex asks, swiftly changing the subject.

I take the distraction gratefully. "I would love to just have a wander around, get a feel for the place if that's okay? And maybe go to the beach…though I have no idea how far away that is. Wait, we don't have a car…" I trail off at my presumption. Maybe all Alex wanted to do was lie by the pool.

"That's not a problem. I have a hire car being delivered here in the next hour so we can go for a bit of a drive…see some sights and then head to the beach later. Does that sound okay?" Alex suggests.

"Awesome," I say, borrowing the word that the Aussies seem to use every five minutes.

Alex gives me a grin, stealing one of my fries as I protest loudly. I finish off my meal and sigh contently. Just then, I hear a chime and Alex looks down at his phone. "Good, the car is here. Did you want to grab some stuff from the room and we can head out?"

"Sounds good to me," I respond.

Back in the room I grab my swimming costume and towel, along with my factor thirty sun cream, and shove them in a bag before picking up my handbag and stuffing in my sunglasses and purse. I meet Alex down in the lobby and take his arm as he guides me out to the hire car. I am not exactly sure what make it is, but it is some kind of high-end 4x4. When I climb inside, it is blissfully cool, making me wonder how people survive without air conditioning in this part of the world.

With the assuredness of someone who has lived somewhere his whole life, Alex takes me on a tour of his city. I marvel at the stories he tells me of his childhood and how things have changed. He takes me to his favourite places, a lot of which seem to be drive-through food places where we grab the most amazing fresh doughnuts I have ever tasted, and he even manages to persuade me to try this iced coffee frappe thing. I thought it was going to be disgusting, but it was sweet and creamy and probably filled with like a million calories. Yeah, I loved it.

All set with our sugar and caffeine fix, Alex tells me we are going to head down to Fremantle. The name rings a bell and I dig out the guidebook that I threw in my bag at the last minute. I read out random facts and soon I have Alex laughing at me being a complete tourist. The trip takes a good couple of hours, making a giant loop that brings us back from Fremantle via South Perth and then into the city itself. I will never forget the view as we came round on the freeway with the river to the side and in front of us and the city off to our right...just breath-taking. We exit the city taking a detour through the botanical gardens, which are nothing like I have ever seen, and then drive out through the suburbs to City Beach.

"This is the best fish and chips you will ever taste," Alex promises me, indicating to the restaurant in front of us. "Let's hit the beach first and then we'll grab some dinner later."

"Cool," I say. "I am not really up for swimming, though, if that's okay?" Truth be told, I am a bit scared of sharks but don't want to admit that to Alex and seem like a complete wuss.

"That's cool...you can just dip your feet in if you

want," Alex replies, a knowing smile on his face.

The sun is a bit lower in the sky now that it is late afternoon, and as we trudge down the sand towards the water's edge, the light shimmers off the water, forcing me to don my sunglasses. I bravely pop my bare foot out, waiting to experience the chill of the water, like you would in the UK. But instead of bone-numbingly freezing, the water is cool and pleasant and I almost wish that I hadn't left my costume in the car. I don't know how long we stand there, both staring out into the ocean, but eventually Alex starts to fidget and suggests we head up to the fish place, Clancy's.

We make our way back up the dunes and round to the entrance, where I brush the sand from my feet and slip on my flip-flops, or thongs as Alex called them. We are shown to a table out on the deck and I can't help but feel like this is the life. Why Aussies want to live in rainy old England when they can have this beats me. Alex and I sit side by side, looking out over the water as we sip our drinks. I noticed the subtle raised brow once again when I ordered only a juice, but Alex doesn't push it. I order the barramundi on Alex's recommendation and Alex orders the hoki, both types of fish completely foreign to me, but I am looking forward to trying them out. We chat amicably until our food arrives and then there is almost complete silence as we taste our meals.

I groan in appreciation at the taste explosion in my mouth, and Alex chuckles next to me. "Good?" he asks.

"Hmm, yum," I respond, taking another bite. Seriously, I have never tasted anything like this and I am not sure I ever will again. We munch through the rest of our meal as we watch the sun slip down closer and closer to the horizon. When at last we are finished, even too stuffed for dessert, Alex suggests just hanging out on the sand to watch the sunset.

We wander down onto the sand again and find a spot. I lean my head against Alex's arm and, almost reflexively, he winds it around me and draws me into his side. The feel of him is so foreign, yet completely familiar, and I simply enjoy sitting as we listen to the waves crashing on the shore. I am so completely lost in my thoughts that I don't even realise that Alex has asked me a question until I feel him nudge me.

"Why don't you drink?" Alex asks softly, his expression searching.

Something about this man seems to compel the truth out of me and I find myself telling Alex things I have never shared with anyone. "My dad," I begin. "Well, he had a bit of a problem with drink, mostly wine actually. He would come home from work and start with a glass, 'to relax' he would say, and then that would turn into a bottle or two. Some nights he would fall asleep in front of the TV, but most nights he would get angry and abusive. Mostly it was just verbal, but every once in a while he would lash out at my mother." I can feel that Alex's posture has gone rigid and I can feel the anger rolling off of him.

"The night after my thirteenth birthday, he got completely trashed. I think it was because he had lost this account at work and had been called into his boss's office and been given a warning. I was going out to a disco with my friends and was about to leave the house when he called me into the front room. He went off on one about how I looked like a slut with my makeup on and how boys were only after one thing. He tried shoving me back towards the stairs to go clean my face and I, in my stupid teenage bravery, told him that I could go out how I liked. I wasn't even wearing much, and my mum had already seen me and said it was fine, so I wasn't about to let him spoil my night. That's when he hit me. He slapped me across the face so hard they thought he had broken my nose. All I really remember is, afterwards, he leant into me, breathing horrible wine fumes into my face, and told me that I was a slut just like my mother and that I had it coming."

"The fucker," Alex says quietly, but I don't look up at him, concentrating on the sun setting on the horizon instead.

"I think that was the last straw. My mother threw him out, threatening him that she would press charges if he came near us again. And that was the last I ever heard from him. After that it was just me and my mother until…" I trail off trying to hold back the emotions I have desperately kept locked inside all these years.

"So when did your mother get diagnosed?" Of course, Alex knows what's wrong with her—he has paid for her treatment after all, I think to myself.

"After my dad left, things were good for a while. Mum and I were really close, but sometimes it seemed more like I was taking care of her rather than the other way round. She was becoming more and more forgetful, living her life by lists, and I was constantly checking that things were turned off. When I was trying to decide what university to go to, I made sure I only chose those in London so that I could still live at home.

"All that time she still managed to work, so financially things were okay, but her boss noticed that her behaviour was getting a little erratic. I was in my second year when I got a call to say she had flipped out on a customer. I think her boss knew something was up with her, but he hadn't wanted to get rid of her. But that day was the last straw, so he called me.

"I managed to get her to see a doctor, but as she was only forty-two, they were reluctant to label her with Alzheimer's. It took me a year of pushing to get a diagnosis, and although it was the worst-case scenario, the relief at finally having an answer was huge."

I am lost in my head as I tell my story; the relief of being able to talk to someone about everything is unreal. "Life carried on, I managed to get my degree and, as luck would have it, I managed to walk into a curatorial role at the London Museum. The money sucked, but I loved my job and for a while things were good. Mum had a carer coming in to check on her, so I knew she was okay during the day. But things got progressively worse, so I then had to get her into a home. At first the money I made was enough, but as the level of care she needed had to be increased, so did the cost, and in the end I had no choice but to sell the house to pay for her care. That lasted a few years, and at least I knew she was getting the best care possible.

"Then, about five years ago, she stopped recognising me. I think that was actually the worst day of my life," I say, unaware that tears are running down my face. "And really it has been downhill ever since. Eventually, my salary was not enough, so I found the job with Charles and left the museum…and the rest you know." For the first time, I turn my head to look up at Alex and I see him regarding me with a dark expression. He reaches across and wipes the tears from beneath my eyes as I take in a deep breath.

"Well, I am here now," Alex states firmly, though his tone is soft. "You are not alone, and you don't have to worry about money again." I go to retort that he will be around for only a year, but I clamp my mouth shut, not wanting to ruin the moment. Instead, I lean my head into Alex's neck and watch the sun completely disappear into the horizon.

Eventually, Alex suggests that we head back to the hotel, and as I get to my feet I realise how tired I am. I barely manage to keep my eyes open through our journey, and when we get back to the suite, I dive into the shower for a quick wash before climbing in between the crisp sheets.

# CHAPTER FIVE

The smell of bacon has me climbing out of bed. I follow my nose and find myself in the living area staring at a table filled with food. A rustle alerts me to Alex's presence on the sofa and I squeak out a startled "Good morning."

"I wondered if you were going to join the land of the living any time soon," Alex says with a smirk across his face. "Dig in. I've already eaten."

Ooh, there is too much choice. My eyes wander over a mound of delectable pastries and a platter of fresh fruit, and I take a moment to lift various cloches where I find the makings of a full English. I pour myself a cup of tea from a pot standing on the side and sip on the steaming brew as I contemplate what I feel like eating. I help myself to a stack of pancakes that I spy, add a couple of crispy rashers of bacon and then pour over some gloriously sticky maple syrup. I settle down on the corner to eat and find myself groaning in appreciation as I take a mouthful. Seriously, this is food heaven. "Oh my god, I am going to be the size of a house if I keep eating like this," I mumble.

Alex looks over at me and runs his eyes over my body. I am suddenly feeling very aware that I am wearing only a pair of tiny cotton shorts and a vest top. "You could do with a few more curves, Liv. It would suit you."

I am startled by Alex's assessment. "Funny, I thought most guys liked skinny girls," I joke half-heartedly, knowing that my lack of curves is the result of stress and not fashion.

"Nah, you want something you can hold on to," Alex says, grinning back at me, and I find myself smiling in response.

Before I can reply, there is a loud knock on the door of the suite. Alex gets up to answer it with a puzzled look on his face; evidently he was not expecting anyone. I am startled when I hear a loud girlish squeal emanating from the direction of the door. Then, without warning, a tiny blonde woman comes barrelling towards me with a huge smile on her face, followed by a beautiful woman who looks about my age and bears a startling resemblance to Alex.

"There she is," the woman says excitedly. "You never told me how beautiful she is, Alex," she admonishes as she comes to stand in front of me.

I glance across at Alex, knowing that I must look like a deer caught in the headlights, but he just gives me a grin and a helpless shrug. It is clear to me that this must be Alex's mother and all I can think of is what a dynamo she is.

"Um. Hi, Mrs Davenport. I am Olivia. Liv, actually," I say, holding my hand out to her. She bypasses the hand and immediately pulls me into an all-encompassing hug. She has a kind of Julie Andrews vibe going on and I immediately find myself relaxing. I have to warn myself not to get complacent. The last thing I need is to get too comfortable and let something slip.

"It's Sheila, darling. No need for formality when you are about to join the family." The way she says the word 'family' combined with the twinkle in her eye makes me wonder if she has some mafia connections somewhere.

"Um, okay, Sheila," I respond as she pulls back

and holds me at arm's length.

"And this here is my daughter, Nadia," Sheila says. Nadia steps forward and gives me a hug, murmuring a breathless 'hello', though it is definitely a little more reserved than her mother's.

"Mum, what's with the ambush?" Alex suddenly asks, and I can hear the tone of a slightly petulant child that only a mother can bring out.

"Oh, hush, Alex. You didn't think you could keep her hidden any longer? I gave you a day, and now it's my turn to find out all about this beautiful girl who has captured your heart." I find myself blushing, and all at once, I feel the guilt of lying to such a lovely woman.

"Mum, come on…" I sense Alex is trying to rescue me, but he is obviously no match for his mother.

"Right, Olivia," Sheila says, "We need to get you dressed and then we are taking you shopping."

I let out a squeak, not sure that I am ready to be left alone with these two women, as lovely as they seem. Plus it is not like I have any money to go shopping with. Sensing my distress Alex intervenes, "Mum, I am not sure Liv is really up for a day of girly shopping."

"Nonsense," Sheila responds. "The girl needs a wedding dress, pronto. You said yourself that she had not found anything she liked in London." I can feel my cheeks growing warm and I know that I need to sit down with Alex at some point and make sure our stories are straight. Alex gives me another helpless shrug and I know that I am trapped.

"Um, shopping sounds good, Sheila," I say. "Can you give me ten to jump in the shower and get into some proper clothes?"

"Sure thing, darling. We'll grab a coffee and catch up with Alex here," Sheila says with a smile, but I sense that poor Alex will be getting a grilling of his own. I catch Nadia's eye. She gives me a conspiratorial grin and I know we are both thinking the same thing.

I head into the master bedroom to take the world's fastest shower before digging through my bag to find something suitable to wear. My wardrobe is meagre, to say the least, but I can just blame the weather in England for the lack of summer clothes. In the end, I come up with a stretchy blue cotton dress, with capped sleeves, that falls just above my knee. It will have to do. I slide my feet into a pair of white sandals, add some gloss and run a brush through my hair. Done. I glance at my watch and realise I have a couple of minutes to spare, so I sit on my bed and take a couple of deep breaths, knowing that today is going to be filled with questions.

When I finally feel mentally prepared, I make my way back into the living area to find Alex lounging on the sofa chatting softly to his mother and sister. They all look up as I enter and I see Alex running his eyes over my body, a smile on his face. It is far from predatory, but it still forces a blush up my neck. Okay, so at least I pass muster.

"Right, time to go shopping," Sheila announces, getting to her feet, and I can definitely see where Alex gets his commanding nature. As I pick up my handbag, Alex comes over to me, wrapping me in a hug. Before I have a chance to do anything he lowers his lips to my ear and murmurs, "Relax. It will be okay. They will ask loads of questions, but the story is we met two months ago at a book auction and fell madly in love. We didn't want to wait, so here we are. Okay?"

I nod my head discreetly and he plants a soft kiss on my cheek. "Have a nice day, Liv. Don't let these two bully you into anything you don't want, okay?" he says louder, for his mother's benefit. I grin up at Alex, grateful for the pep talk. Out of nowhere, Alex produces a small black credit card. "Here you go, sweetheart. Charge everything to this. There is no limit, so go wild. The pin is your birthday." Alex gives me a broad smile. Holy shit. A card with no limit...wow. I can't even fathom that. But before I have a chance to say anything else, I am being ushered out the door by two women with a purpose.

I lose track of the wedding dress boutiques we visit, but as I try on dress after dress, I just can't find anything that works. I know this is not my dream wedding but I still want to be comfortable, and in this heat I am sure I am going to melt in the meringues that I try on. Sheila and Nadia are patient with me, but I sense that I had better choose something soon or we are all going to get a bit fed up.

We are back in the city on the main shopping street and Nadia suggests a break for lunch making me grateful for the distraction. As I chew on my panini, Nadia and Sheila reflect on the dresses that I tried on, trying to persuade me on their favourites. The real issue for me, though, was the cost of the dresses. Tens of thousands of dollars. I just could not feel comfortable spending that amount on a dress that I will wear once. That is like a deposit on a house, or university tuition, or even a really fancy car. To spend it on a dress just seems crazy.

We are just heading back out onto the street when a dress in one of the windows catches my eye. I drag my companions over as I look at the display critically. "I want to try that one on," I declare, pointing at a strapless ivory and cream lace cocktail dress. The design is simple but beautiful. I hurry inside and ask the assistant if they have that dress in my size.

I know the instant I step out of the changing cubicle that this is the one. Both ladies have a gleam in their eye and admiration on their faces. And even better, the dress is only a couple hundred dollars, which is much more acceptable to me. "Do you think Alex will like it?" I ask shyly and Sheila smiles at me with a nod. "Then this is the one, guys," I declare, before stepping back into the changing room to put on my clothes.

When I emerge a few minutes later, I see Nadia clutching a pair of shoes that go with the dress, and at her suggestion, I try them on. I soon have the women giggling at my attempts to walk in the sky-high heels. The assistant is my saviour when she brings out a second pair in the same design but with a lower heel. Satisfied with my purchases, I ask the girl to ring them up, having only a minor heart attack when I realise the shoes cost almost the same as the dress. I hand over the little plastic rectangle that Alex gave me and I breathe a sigh of relief when the sale goes through. Old habits die hard, I guess.

"Right, now we need to do something with your hair, darling," Sheila declares, and I find myself bringing up a hand to my unruly mop. I am about to argue with her, but Sheila thwarts me by telling me she has already booked me an appointment. Not wanting to let her down, I allow myself to be walked down to an airy salon where Sheila takes charge.

As I sit in the chair, I think back over the morning and realise that it has actually been fun. I have not had that kind of mother-daughter bonding for such a long time, and immediately I feel swamped by guilt that I am lying to these two lovely people. I look over to the nail bar, where Sheila and Nadia are both getting mani-pedis, chatting away, and I feel a stab of envy shoot through me at their closeness. Whatever Alex's secret is, I can't see how he thinks that his family wouldn't support him; they seem so close-knit.

The hairdresser mumbles behind me, saying that it looks like I have cut my hair myself, and I find myself blushing because that is exactly what I have been doing. When you don't have the money, monthly trips to get your hair cut aren't an option. I watch in alarm as the hairdresser chops into the back of my hair with ferocity, but he assures me it needs to be done to sort out the uneven layers. The front, however, he leaves long around my chin, all the while blending it into the back so that I now have an elegant angled bob that frames my face. A quick blow-dry later and I feel like a new woman.

I join Nadia and Sheila for my own mani-pedi and soon they are regaling me with childhood stories about Alex. At one point I am laughing so hard the tears leak from my eyes, and I find myself wondering when the last time I actually had fun was.

It is late afternoon when we finally head back to the hotel, laden down with bags, though the majority are not mine. Alex texts me to meet in the beer garden, so we drop the bags in the room and then head out to find him lazing in the sun with a cold beer. The ladies order a jug of sangria while I stick to a lime and soda and some sharing snacks.

I find myself blushing when Alex compliments my new haircut, running his fingers through the short tendrils at the back and then tucking a stray lock behind my ear. I can see Sheila is watching us carefully so push through my nerves and plant a light kiss on Alex's cheek as I whisper a 'thank you' in his ear.

"So, did you find the one?" Alex asks and I hear the jest in his tone.

"Yup," I answer. "Shoes too." I am sure Alex is probably not that interested in my shopping expedition, so instead I ask him about his day.

"This and that," he answers evasively, but not wanting to intrude, I leave it at that.

Our drinks and snacks arrive and we dig in, but not before Sheila digs out a notepad from her purse and starts quizzing us on the wedding arrangements. Given that I actually have no idea what's going on, I leave it to Alex to answer.

It turns out that we are to be married at the family's vineyard in three days' time and the reception will be held in the restaurant that they own there as well. It seems like everything is in hand and I happily go along with the menu suggestions that Sheila puts forward. The only hiccup comes when Sheila grills me about who is coming from my side and I have to admit that no one will be attending. We gloss over my father, but when I tell her about my mother I see tears form in Sheila's eyes and, before I know it, I am being given one of her hugs. I pat her on the back and let her know that it's okay, and she firmly tells me that I am to think of the Davenports as family now.

When Sheila and Nadia are satisfied that

everything 'wedding' is in hand, the notebook goes back into the bag and they start chatting about family relations instead. I have a hard time keeping track of who is who, so I just sit back and listen to the gossip, enjoying the sense of serenity surrounding me.

I am startled when Alex suddenly looks at his watch and suddenly announces that it is time for us to go. "What do you mean?" I ask. I am shattered from our shopping expedition and not really in the mood to go out.

"I have a surprise for you, Liv. Come on, we need to get going. We have to get there before sunset," Alex says with a twinkle in his eye.

"Okay, right…" I trail off. "Do I need to change?" I ask, hoping that Alex is not going to suddenly want to go clubbing or something.

"Nope, just as you are is fine. Come on, we need to get a wriggle on." Alex gets up and holds his hand out to me, giving me a wink. Clearly Sheila and Nadia are in on the surprise because they tell us to get out of here and get going. We say our goodbyes and I thank them once again for a fabulous day.

Minutes later we are in the car headed up the highway with Alex refusing to tell me where we are going. For the most part the journey is silent, the radio providing the backdrop to our easy companionship. I break the silence when I suddenly get an attack of the giggles at the name on one of the road signs. Alex looks at me quizzically. "Innaloo. Seriously, there is a place here called In..a..loo? I am imagining a giant toilet here, you know!" Alex bursts out laughing and for a few minutes neither us can talk, we are laughing so hard.

"I never thought of it like that," chuckles Alex. A

short while later we head off the highway and then pull into an entrance sign-posted 'Pinnaroo Valley Memorial Park'. Okay, so this is a bit bizarre, but I am sure Alex has his reasons for bringing me to a cemetery. I am pretty sure that Sheila had mentioned that all of Alex's grandparents were still alive, but maybe he has another reason. Alex drives for a few minutes and then pulls into a parking space alongside a vast expanse of lawn.

We climb out of the car and I follow Alex as he strolls along the tree line and then crosses onto the grass. I can see that back on the other side of the road are cemetery plots. Mostly I am looking at a colossal graveyard, I surmise to myself, but it is unlike those that I am used to back home in the UK with the large headstones. Instead, the markers are mostly inlaid into the grass, and the flowers and the wreaths seem to be made of plastic. Alex leads us to a bench and motions for us to sit down. I am about to start questioning Alex when he puts his finger to his lips, motioning to be quiet, before pointing into a tree line.

I squint hard and just then catch some motion. I am holding my breath when I notice a mob of about ten kangaroos hopping out onto the grass. They seem completely oblivious to our presence and now I realise why Alex has been so quiet. We watch as they graze on the grass in front of us, gradually drifting closer and closer. I can see joeys in their mothers' pouches, and Alex quietly points out the males in the group. The scene in front of me is so unexpected and I can't help but squeeze Alex's hand to stop myself from squealing out loud. He looks at me with a satisfied smile and I realise that my reaction has made him happy.

We sit like that for a good hour, watching the various family groups come and go, as the sun sets. When it is almost completely dark Alex motions for us to head back to the car. "Wow, Alex. That was just...amazing. I have never seen anything like that before," I exclaim once we are back inside the vehicle.

"A nice surprise then?" he asks.

"The best, thank you. Definitely one to cross off the bucket list," I respond, a smile stretching across my face. I stare out the window as we head back onto the highway, completely lost in my thoughts. So much so that I miss Alex asking if I want to go for something to eat.

"Would you mind if we head back to the hotel?" I ask. "Your mum kind of wore me out with all that shopping today and I am still stuffed from the snacks we had earlier. I think I really just need to head to bed."

"Sure thing," Alex responds good-naturedly. "Look, was everything okay today? My mum didn't give you too much of a hard time, did she? I know she can be a bit intense..." Alex continues, looking a little uncomfortable.

"Not at all," I reassure him. "Your mum and sister were both lovely. We had a great time. Plus I managed to actually get a dress that didn't cost the GDP of a third world country." At that, Alex bursts out laughing, and I find myself filling him in on some of the crazier dresses that Sheila insisted I try on.

By the time that I have showered and curled under the sheets in my bed, I am fit to drop. Today has been awesome and I find myself wondering how I got so lucky. Okay, this might be an arranged marriage, a business transaction, but spending a year with Alex will certainly be no hardship. I close my eyes, remembering the kangaroos, and fall asleep with a smile on my face.

# CHAPTER SIX

The next couple of days fly by and before I know it my wedding day is here. I stare at myself in the mirror and take in the sight of myself. My hair has been swept up at the front and styled to include a beautifully delicate silver headband studded with tiny turquoise crystals. My makeup is subtle with that 'barely there' look that takes a thousand layers to achieve. And my dress is like a second skin, hugging my body and giving me curves where I was lacking.

I know I have only a few minutes before I need to make my ways downstairs, and I have to force myself to take a couple of deep breaths to calm myself. Despite Alex's intention of us staying at the hotel, Sheila nearly had a fit when he told her and she insisted that the night before the wedding we would be staying in the family home—separate bedrooms of course, which made us chuckle.

In a feeble attempt at distracting myself, I think back to what it was like meeting Alex's family yesterday. The first thing that hit me as we walked through the front door was that chaos and noise reigned supreme, and it took a couple of minutes before anyone even noticed us standing there in the hallway with our small overnight bags. Moments later I was being swept into a giant bear hug by a man who could only be Alex's dad. With the insistence of calling him Bruce, I was then passed around the family members as we made our introductions.

For the most part Alex had made sure I was briefed on his mum and dad; two older brothers, Chris and Luke; and his sister, Nadia, whom I had already met. I had spent hours poring over the details that Alex had included in the summary of each of his grandparents, parents and siblings, their respective partners and children included, so I felt like I knew my way around the family tree. That, combined with the Facebook stalking I had done—well, if you have an open profile, what do you expect?—had made me feel more confident about meeting this tight-knit family. Research has always been my default setting when faced with the unknown and I had indeed researched the shit out of the family I was about to join.

What those hours of research had not prepared me for, however, was the love that seemed to flow throughout the house. From the gentle teasing to the all-out banter, this was the kind of family I had always envied growing up. As the day wore on and I got to know everyone a little better and they in turn interrogated me until Alex stepped in to rescue me with a tour of the estate, I finally felt accepted. Something which terrified the living shit out of me, given that I was basically lying to their faces.

It wasn't until I had curled up in bed later that night that I finally let go and quietly sobbed into my pillow. My part in this deception would surely come back to haunt me, no matter how much Alex and I tried to justify it.

So here I am, in a beautifully appointed guestroom, waiting to become Mrs Alexander Davenport. I hear a gentle rap at the door and Nadia pokes her head around the door to let me know everyone is ready. With a final, fortifying, breath I make my way out of the room and come face to face with Bruce, Alex's dad. Despite his appearance of a giant, Bruce is actually a teddy bear at heart, a fact I discovered as I watched him dote on his grandchildren. Emily, Nadia's youngest, in particular has him wrapped around her little finger.

"Liv, you look beautiful," Bruce says in his gruff voice with a twinkle in his eye.

"Thank you, Bruce," I reply with a smile. "And you look rather spiffy yourself."

"Argh, this is a monkey suit," he responds, tugging on his shirt collar. "Listen, love, I know you don't have your old man here, but I wondered if you would like me to walk you down the aisle. I know it won't be the same, and you haven't known us long…" Bruce trails off, clearly uncomfortable.

"Thank you, Bruce. That would be lovely," I reply softly, trying to hold back the tears in my eyes. "I would really appreciate that." And I actually do. The thought of having to walk down the aisle all by myself has brought me out in a cold sweat several times already.

"All right then. Let's get this show on the road," says Bruce, offering me his arm.

Before I know it, I am standing at the top of the aisle in the beautiful spot that is commonly used for wedding ceremonies on the property, surveying the scene before me. Guests have filled the covered chairs that sit either side of the red carpet that I am about to walk up. At the bottom of the aisle is a shady pavilion, amongst a few large eucalyptus trees, where I will be saying my vows. The music is indicating that it is time to move, but my feet feel glued to the floor. A small nudge from Bruce and a whispered 'Just one foot in front of the other, love' gets me moving. My eyes are on Alex, who smiles encouragingly at me from the pavilion. As I make my way down the aisle, I can feel everyone else's eyes on me as well, and I chant Bruce's words over and over in my head until I am standing at the front with Alex.

I am in a bit of a dream as I say my vows. The nerves in my belly have entirely disappeared, and in the abstract I wonder what it is about Alex that makes me feel so calm. He should bottle the stuff. When, finally, all is said and we have exchanged our simple platinum bands, I finally hear the words that I have been dreading: "You may now kiss the bride." For the last few days, it has been bothering me that I would have to kiss Alex in front of everyone. Granted, Alex has actually been quite touchy-feely and affectionate in front of everyone, but this will be our actual first kiss.

As Alex stares down at me, my breath hitches and I know he can sense my nerves. Then he lowers his lips onto mine and the world recedes. The kiss is gentle as his lips meld against mine. I feel his arms go around my waist as he pulls me closer into his body. Without thinking, my arms wind around his neck of their own accord and the kiss deepens as my mouth parts slightly. Taking the cue, Alex slips his tongue into my mouth and suddenly a hunger takes over as he growls softly into my mouth.

A cheer suddenly brings us both back to the present and I feel my cheeks flame with embarrassment. Seriously, making out at your wedding is a little crass. Alex grabs my hand and plants a kiss on my palm before turning and pulling me up the aisle. "Photographs," he murmurs, reminding me that we would be going around to the vineyard's lake to have our official pictures taken. We wait for the shower of confetti to finish before jumping into the 4x4 waiting to take us on our short journey.

"You okay?" Alex asks, putting an arm around my trembling frame.

"Yeah, it's just the adrenaline. It's not every day you get married," I joke, and I see a strange expression cross Alex's face.

"You look very beautiful, Liv," Alex says seriously.

"Um, th…thank you," I stutter, not sure what else to say. Do I compliment him on his suit? In the end, I don't say anything else and just sit back and wait as we wind our way to the lake.

The setting is beautiful and it is a relief to have some private time after the scrutiny I have been under for the last few days. I am exhausted by the questions and trying to make sure that I have kept my story straight, and my heart breaks a little each time I lie to these amazing people. The photographer walks off to set up his equipment and Alex turns to me, pulling me into his embrace as we maintain our façade.

"Thank you, Liv," he says softly.

"For what?" I ask, raising an eyebrow.

"For being the perfect bride. For being so gracious. And for making my family so happy. I know this is probably not what either of us envisioned for our wedding days, but I am being completely honest when I say that I couldn't have asked for a better partner in crime." Alex breaks out a grin, lightening the mood, and I find myself grinning back.

"Well, we have pulled it off, so now just the reception to go…" I add.

We pose for what feels like ages, but in reality it's only about half an hour before we head back to the restaurant. When we are arrive, I am overwhelmed by the beauty of the spot. The building is a traditional tin-roof construction with a wide wrap-around deck. The inside is cool in the heat, but the large open doors allow the air to flow through. Long tables are covered in pristine white linens and delicate glassware, a gorgeous contrast to the dark wooden chairs. Alex loops his arm through mine and gently guides me up to the top table as we are surrounded by applause. He pauses only to drop a kiss on my lips before pulling out my chair. If any of this were actually real, I think I would probably swoon.

The remainder of the day passes in somewhat of a blur. The dinner, the speeches, the dancing and the socialising are all perfect, but it is a relief when eight o'clock rolls around and Alex lets me know our car is here. Once we have made our final farewells it feels liberating to slip into the cool quiet of the limo, knowing that I can finally let my guard down.

"So back to London then?" I say, realising in all of this I had completely forgotten about what would happen after we actually got married.

"Nope," says Alex, rubbing the bridge of his nose. I take in the circles under his eyes and realise today has been a strain for him as well. "No, I think we both deserve a bit of a holiday after all that. So we are off to Bali for a week."

"What?" I screech, and Alex looks at me, confusion in his features.

"Sorry about that. I mean, seriously? I have always dreamt about going to Bali. It's actually on my bucket list," I say

"Then I picked right," Alex confirms with a smile. The air conditioning in the car is up a little too high and goosebumps break out across my skin, causing me to shiver. Seeing this, Alex winds his arm around me and pulls me into his warmth. I lay my head on his shoulder, relaxing for the first time in days, and think to myself how lucky I am. This may be a marriage of convenience, but Alex is such a good man and I could do far worse than spending a year with this generous and kind guy. But I know I need to be careful and guard my heart because falling in love with him would be the biggest mistake ever. Despite the closeness we have, Alex has shown no sign in finding me the least bit attractive, and I am sure he chose me only because of my desperate situation.

# CHAPTER SEVEN

Our time in Bali is magical for me. When we finally walked into our villa—the presidential suite, no less—after a moderately long flight and transfer, I was fit to drop. Yet the moment I stood on the patio overlooking the Indian Ocean, my exhaustion lifted completely and poor Alex had to watch me squeal with excitement as I explored every corner of the suite. Luxurious is not an adequate description of the villa. I mean, there is a bar complete with pool table and a grand piano, for heaven's sake. Once again, Alex insisted I take the master bedroom and I had only a moment of guilt before happily accepting and bouncing on the enormous bed like a five-year-old.

For the last few days, we have simply relaxed, enjoying our private infinity pool and even making use of the spa. In the short time, my relationship with Alex has developed and I would actually go so far as to say that we are friends. Weird, I know, but when I agreed to marry him, the last thing I had expected was friendship. I have discovered that we have very similar tastes in books and movies and we have spent endless hours chatting about our favourite characters. Alex is also attempting to teach me chess, but I am hopeless and he keeps beating me in only a couple of moves; I have found that he is an excellent strategist. However, I did manage to hustle him at pool, much to his annoyance and my delight.

The villa is so self-contained we have barely set foot outside, but tomorrow, Alex has told me, he has a surprise in store for me. I am lying on one of the comfortable sunbeds on our private patio set high up on the cliff, gazing out at the sunrise, when I hear footsteps behind me. I turn my head to find Alex next to me, wordlessly holding out a mug of tea and wearing nothing but a pair of shorts. This has become somewhat of a morning ritual, me rising with the dawn and him bringing a steaming brew for me and a coffee for himself while we watch the sun rise together in silence.

Not for the first time do I take the time to appreciate his beautiful body. Years of surfing, running and daily gym visits have honed his frame, giving him muscles in all the right places and a washboard stomach that you could bounce a penny off. The first time I saw him in swim shorts I nearly had a heart attack; never in my life had I been in the vicinity of such male perfection, and I was glad to already be in the pool so that he wouldn't know how wet he made me. Lusting after Alex is definitely not part of our agreement, and each time I start to think about him in that way, I have to remind myself that he definitely doesn't think that way about me. Yet each time he brushes my arm or plants one of his frequent kisses on my head, I have to stop my heart from beating a little faster and remind myself that Alex is just being affectionate and that things are purely platonic. But I guess that doesn't stop the daydreams…shit, I have this bad.

When the sun has finally made its way above the horizon, I go to stand and am instantly doubled over by a sharp pain streaking through my pelvis. I must have let out a squeak because instantly Alex is at my side asking me if I am okay.

"I'm fine," I gasp.

"Well, clearly you are not okay," Alex retorts, an

eyebrow raised.

"It's just girl stuff, Alex. Nothing for you to worry about. Okay?" I try to straighten up again but am instantly hit with another bolt of pain, which has me crying out, and I actually feel dizzy. I have been on the pill for years to regulate my periods and ease the agonising cramps I get, and on the whole it works. Well, apart from the odd occasion like this.

Before I can say anything else, Alex mutters "Bullshit" and sweeps me into his arms, carrying me through to my bedroom and laying me on the bed. The cramps are all consuming now, running through my back and down my legs, and I find myself curling up into the foetal position, trying to breathe through the pain. I am not even aware that Alex had left the room until he is back, crouched down in front of me with a glass of water and a couple of painkillers in his hand, his eyes filled with concern. I accept them gratefully, hoping that they will ease the pain soon; I am not sure just how much more I can take. My eyes are closed as I try to focus on breathing...in and out...in and out. The bed dips behind me and the next thing that I feel are Alex's warm hands on my lower back, rubbing firm circles.

It takes about fifteen minutes for the painkillers to kick in and take the edge off the pain and I am finally able to uncurl myself from my position. With gentle hands, Alex helps me to roll over and then wipes the tears from my eyes. "Are you okay, Liv?" he asks.

"Getting there," I say softly. The pain is dull now, thrumming through my body like I have run a marathon, and I feel exhausted. "Sorry, Alex. It's not normally like that. Just every once in a while..." I trail off, feeling embarrassed discussing 'women's things' with him.

"Don't apologise, Liv. Just rest now, okay? Those painkillers are probably going to knock you out, so close your eyes and let your body recover."

"Okay," I murmur as the sleepiness takes over and I succumb to black nothingness.

I wake to find my head groggy and feeling like it is stuffed with cotton wool, to find the sun has set and, miraculously, I am pain-free. I glance around to find Alex seated on a chair watching me intently, with the strangest look on his face. "Hey," I murmur, wondering if he has been in my room the entire time I have been asleep.

"Hey. How are you feeling?" Alex asks.

"Much better, thanks. A little woolly-headed but no cramps, thank god," I respond. My stomach lets out the loudest growl, making me laugh, and Alex quickly reaches out for the phone and requests for our dinner to be brought up immediately.

"Does everyone just do as you ask?" I joke, and Alex just shrugs in response. This is something I have teased him mercilessly about; when Alex Davenport says jump, people ask how high. Feeling hot and sticky with the humidity I tell Alex that I want to have a shower. The odd look returns to his face, but he just nods and leaves me to it.

*~*~*~*

The roar of the engines fills my ears and I grip the arms of my seat until my knuckles turn white. It is not that I am scared of flying per se, but I really just don't like the feeling of take-offs and landings. Without a word, Alex takes my hand and gently strokes my skin with his thumb. The physical contact instantly soothes me and I close my eyes, directing my thoughts back to my surprise trip to the elephant sanctuary as a distraction.

We had left the resort before sunrise in a taxi, which had taken several hours to drive us up into the mountains. Driving past the rice paddies, I felt like I had been transported into another world and I had to remind myself that the luxury that Alex surrounds himself with is a dream for most.

Our day was spent interacting with the elephants at the safari park, washing a beautiful, and very patient, female, feeding the babies and watching the talent show. At dusk, we went on an elephant-back safari through the forest, where I found myself hanging on to Alex for dear life as I tried to get used to the elephant's unusual gait. Upon our return, we ended up eating in the park's restaurant overlooking the lake with a view of the elephants getting ready for bed. It truly was one of the most amazing experiences of my life and I find myself smiling at the memories.

"What are you thinking of?" Alex whispers in my ear, making me jump.

"Oh, I was just remembering our trip up to Taro to see the elephants. It was so awesome! I still can't thank you enough for that."

"I am just glad you enjoyed it." The plane has now levelled out and Alex has taken his hand back, and I suddenly feel bereft by the lack of his touch.

The rest of the journey is smooth, but gradually, I see a change in Alex as the hours wear on. He has mostly been silent, but as we come into land, his pensive expression becomes colder and colder. The descent into Heathrow is turbulent as bad weather lashes down on us and I find myself clutching the armrests once again. But this time Alex doesn't take my hand. Instead, I notice him grasping onto his own armrests in a vice-like hold. His jaw is locked and his eyes hooded, and all at once I feel like I am sitting next to a complete stranger.

# CHAPTER EIGHT

The rain beats down the side of the bus and I shiver in my coat, despite the heat blasting out through the heaters. Despite being back in London for over a week now, my body still hasn't re-acclimatised to the December weather after the glorious sunshine I have been used to. Lost in my memories of Bali and riding elephants in the reserve, I almost miss my stop, but thankfully someone else rings the bell, breaking me out of my reverie.

I hurry through the rain as I make the short walk home along the square, the park beside me completely invisible in the inclement weather. I finally make it to the front door, where I hurriedly let myself in. As I hang up my dripping coat and stow my umbrella away, I am aware of the silence of the house and wonder whether Alex will make it back tonight.

Each night since we got back, I have made him dinner and waited up with no success. And every morning when I wake the dinner has been placed in the fridge uneaten. On the flight back to London, it was like the easy-going, friendly guy I had got to know just vanished, and in his place I was now living with the steely-eyed man I met at the auction instead. I am not sure what precipitated the change, but life feels very different from the easy-going friendship that we had whilst we were away.

I am about to make my way up to the top floor, where I have my own suite of rooms, when I notice the door down to the basement is slightly ajar. My breath quickens as the memory returns of Alex telling me, quite sternly, on our arrival that I was not to go down there under any circumstances. Truthfully, if he had never said anything, I would have probably never even thought about venturing down into a dark, dank basement, but something about his tone made me curious. Until now the door has been firmly locked with an electronic combination pad, but seeing it open makes me want to go down and see what exactly Alex has been hiding.

After a couple moments of hesitation, I decide to hell with it and push the door open quietly. I listen carefully to work out whether anyone is down there, but I hear nothing. I make my way down the dark stairs, not sure about what I am expecting to see. Alex has hinted about his alternative lifestyle and I sense the basement is linked to this, but really, the word 'alternative' could mean anything. By the time I reach the bottom step I am in pitch darkness. I put out my hand and immediately find a switch, which I flick on.

Soft light illuminates the room and it takes me a few minutes to comprehend what I am looking at. The room must run the length of the house and is open plan, so I step forward trying to grasp what I am actually looking at. The walls are a deep crimson, giving the place a womb-like feeling. In a corner stands a giant wooden cross with what looks like restraints set into it. On one wall I see racks holding whips, canes of various sizes and even what I recognise to be a bullwhip. Holy shit! In the centre of the room is a raised platform, about the size of a bed, covered in a silky-looking throw. Against the far wall is a large leather couch and dotted around are low benches and stools. In the farthest corner, I see a shower cubicle with a couple of robes hung up on the wall.

My subconscious is screaming a word over and over in my mind: BDSM. What the hell? I am no innocent...I read enough, but this is beyond my comprehension. Suddenly a noise behind me startles me and I whip my head around.

"What the hell are you doing down here?" Alex growls at me, his voice filled with ice.

"Uh, uh, the door was open," I say, my face flushing with shame, knowing that I have been caught out.

"I told you not to come down here," Alex states harshly, running a hand through his hair in agitation.

I stare at my feet. "Sorry," I say quietly. "So this is the big secret?" I ask. "Why didn't you just tell me? I am not an idiot, you know." I shudder slightly as I cast my eye around the room, and Alex catches the motion, causing his already explosive face to darken further.

"Does this disgust you?" he hisses into my face so forcefully that I find myself having to take a step back.

"I...I don't know what to think," I say truthfully. "So you hit women. Is that your thing?" I can suddenly understand why Alex would not want his family to know about this. Sheila Davenport is such a strong, independent woman and I am not sure how she would handle the knowledge that her son smacks girls around for fun.

Alex towers over me and I find myself shrinking back. The Alex I knew in Australia would never hurt me, but this one...this one I am not so sure about. "No one who comes here does it unwillingly," Alex states bluntly. I find my eyes drawn to his and when I stare into their depths I can see honesty shining back at me, along with pleading, as if he is subconsciously begging me to understand. I don't doubt his self-belief in whatever he has convinced himself of, but I begin to question every word he has told me to this point.

I find myself so overwhelmed that I cannot think straight, so I run, pushing past Alex, straight up to my room. I am out of breath when I finally slam the door shut behind me, sinking to the ground. The images of everything down in that room play over and over in my mind as I try to process it all, including the change in Alex's demeanour. I wait for clarity, but it never comes.

# CHAPTER NINE

I sit in the pew of the crematorium at Hendon Cemetery as the celebrant begins the service. As I look at my mother's coffin, I can't help but be glad that death claimed her in the way it did, silently in her sleep. An early morning phone call a week ago let me know that she had suffered a massive stroke during the night.

In truth, her death has been a bit of a relief; her quality of life had been deteriorating over the last couple of years and Alzheimer's had stripped her of the person she was. Instead, the woman I had been visiting the last few years was convinced she was eighteen and she had the mouth of a sailor. The mother I knew actually disappeared a long time ago, and even though I have had time to mourn that loss, the grief still bites, opening up the scar that I thought had long since healed.

A sound startles me and then a body is sliding into the seat next to me. I don't have to look up to know that it is Alex.

"I thought you were in America?" I whisper. Since our encounter in the basement a couple weeks ago, we haven't spoken, communicating solely through notes and email about mundane household things. The day before my mother died, Alex flew out to the States on business and was supposed to be there for another ten days. I hadn't wanted to bother him about the funeral, so I didn't tell him about her death, but obviously someone else did.

Alex doesn't reply and simply laces his fingers through mine in a gesture of support. I sit through the service in silence as the celebrant talks about my mother's life, focusing on the good memories I supplied of her and glossing over her disease. There are not many people in attendance, but more than I would have thought, which fills me with a kind of bittersweet sadness.

When the service is finally over, we make our way out into the weak December sunshine. Christmas is just a few days away, and while it would normally be raining this time of year, I am glad for the pleasant day, which I know my mother would have appreciated. I feel empty as people gather around me to express their condolences. I try to accept them as gracefully as possible, but all I really want to do is escape. Alex remains a solid presence next to me, his hand resting gently on my back. Sensing my unease, Alex suggests heading home, seemingly aware that I have not organised a wake. I nod silently and let him guide me to his car, vaguely wondering when he went home to collect it.

I close my eyes the minute I fasten my seat belt to avoid conversation, and I am grateful that Alex just lets me be. My mother's death might be somewhat of a relief, but I still feel sad and incredibly lonely. She may not have been much of a mother to me in recent years, but I can still remember the memories we created together when I was younger.

The moment the car stops I am out the door and straight up to my suite before Alex even has a chance to follow. I just can't stand the idea of making idle chit-chat and I have a headache brewing that I know I just need to sleep off. I pull off my funeral dress, a black and sombre affair that I had tried to cheer up with a fuchsia flower, and pull on a pair of fleecy pyjamas, despite the fact it is only four in the afternoon, and with that, I curl under the covers and wait dry-eyed for sleep to claim me.

*~*~*~*

I am vaguely aware that I am screaming, but I can't work out if it is part of the nightmare that I am trapped in or for real. Suddenly the covers come up and the bed dips as a warm body encircles me.

"Shh. It's okay, Liv. I got you," Alex whispers in my ear, as he strokes my hair off my face and rubs circles over my back. My eyes are still closed as I relive the nightmare of watching my mother die in a hundred horrible ways. I struggle for consciousness, and when I finally open my eyes, I see Alex looking down at me, his face filled with concern. It is the last straw and I break down into great, heaving sobs in his arms. I don't know how long I lie there for, crying in his arms, but he never lets go…never stops the soothing whispers in my ear. Eventually, the tears abate and Alex runs gentle thumbs under my eyes before planting a soft kiss on my forehead. Still circling me, he rolls me over so that he is spooning me, a strong arm wrapped around my waist. "Sleep," he murmurs. "You are safe with me." And I have never felt safer than now, in Alex's arms. Within moments, at his command, I sink into a deep, dreamless sleep.

# CHAPTER TEN

Christmas and New Year's are set to fly by in a whirl of parties. There have been several events already that have demanded my presence, so I have had to dress up and play the dutiful wife. Christmas Day itself, however, is set to be relatively quiet, a rare day when it is just the two of us. I had thought that Alex would resume his business trip to the States, but he insisted he had too much work to do in London. Secretly, I think he wanted to keep an eye on me.

I wake on Christmas Day, surprised to see snowflakes falling outside my window. I pull on my thick purple chenille robe and slippers and make my way quietly down to the kitchen to make myself a cup of tea. I think surprise is written all over my face when I walk in to find Alex flipping pancakes, with bacon sizzling in a pan on the side. "Morning. Happy Christmas," I say softly.

"Merry Christmas, Liv," Alex replies, a cheeky grin stretching across his face, reminding me so much of Aussie Alex. He pours me a cup from a pot of tea standing on the side and I take it gratefully, wandering through to the sunroom that extends into the garden to watch the snow. The house is bare of decorations—I hardly felt like it in the wake of my mother's death–but with the snow falling, it does actually feel a little festive.

"Breakfast is ready," Alex calls out, and I walk back through, taking a seat at the small kitchen table as Alex lays down a plate piled with pancakes and bacon, my absolute favourite breakfast. He hands me the maple syrup with a knowing smile and I pour it over my stack. Alex joins me and we tuck into our food. For the first time since we left Bali, I feel truly comfortable in his presence. I don't know what exactly has changed since the night he climbed into my bed and held me as I cried, but Alex seems more relaxed and chilled.

When every last mouthful has been eaten, Alex declares that we need to Skype with his folks. I run upstairs to grab a shower and make myself presentable before making my way back to the living room with my small pile of presents for Alex. I have not actually spoken to Alex's family since we got back to London, but we have exchanged emails, and Sheila sent me a beautiful card after my mother died. So I am looking forward to catching up and getting a glimpse of how the Davenports celebrate Christmas.

When I enter the living room, I see a decorated tree has magically appeared overnight, along with a large mound of presents. I add my own small pile to the stack and make my way over to Alex, who is busy setting up the laptop to link into the TV. Within moments, I am looking at Sheila and Bruce's living room, which is carnage; paper is strewn all over the place, and kids are screaming and chasing each other. Sheila laughs, and as I take in the scene of family togetherness, I feel tears forming in my eyes. Everyone joins Sheila on the couch to wish us a merry Christmas, but it is not long before the kids get bored and wander off, so we chat for a few minutes before signing off ourselves.

"Presents!" Alex declares, diving for the tree.

"Hmm, I am guessing you like Christmas then?" I ask with a laugh.

"How can you not love Christmas?" Alex

responds, causing me to chuckle. He hands me several boxes before grabbing a few that are obviously for him, the superhero wrapping paper a definite giveaway. "Mum sent these over for us," he says when I raise my eyebrow questioningly.

I open my packages to find a beautiful silk scarf in a vibrant teal colour, a new purse and a gorgeous long cream cardigan that I admired on our shopping trip all that time ago. My eyes well up at Sheila's thoughtfulness. Christmas, for the last five years, had been a solitary affair. I would visit my mother in the morning, taking her some gifts, but she never recognised me and I would always leave feeling depressed. The rest of the day would be spent eating pizza and watching crappy TV, avoiding all the sappy feel-good holiday films.

"You okay?" Alex says, bumping his shoulder with mine playfully.

"All good," I sniff. "Your mum is amazing," I say. "I can't believe she sent me these. She is so thoughtful." I look over at Alex's pile and laugh when I see a jar of Vegemite, a packet of Tim Tams and a pair of boxers with the Australian flag on them.

"Yeah, thoughtful…"Alex sniggers.

Shyly, I hand Alex the small pile of gifts that I got him. "Sorry, it is not much…" I trail off. I really struggled on what to buy him, especially when Alex probably has the means to buy a third world country. Despite Alex giving me an allowance, which I haven't actually touched, I made sure I used the money I made from my job with Charles to pay for these.

Alex rips open the paper and pulls out the soft grey cashmere scarf that I found when I was out and about the week before. I had noticed he didn't seem to have one, so when I came across this one, the exact colour of his eyes, I thought it would suit him. His presents also include an e-reader with a couple of titles that I thought he would like already loaded and a selection of Aussie sweets that I managed to find in one of those random stores that seem to cater to every nationality who might be missing their favourite foods from home.

"I hope that you like them…?" I ask hesitantly.

Alex leans over and gives me a soft kiss on the cheek. "They are lovely. Thank you. You really didn't need to." I shrug in embarrassment but refrain from saying anything more. "Your turn," he says, handing me a stack of boxes.

"What on earth, Alex?" I ask, and this time it is Alex shrugging his shoulders. I open my presents slowly, savouring my gifts. A few of the packages are filled with clothes and I am guessing Alex must have got some assistant, or his secretary, to help him out because he has my size spot on and everything coordinates. "Are you fed up with my fab style already?" I joke.

"Nope, just thought that most chicks are into clothes, and you haven't really been buying anything…" he trails off, looking a little uneasy.

"Thanks, Alex. These are lovely." The rest of the parcels contain perfume, chocolates, a couple of books and even a voucher for a spa day. The items are really personal yet Alex has got each one spot on, making me wonder if he has been going through my things. I dismiss the thought and lean across to give him a kiss, murmuring a soft 'Thank you'.

The rest of the day is spent cooking Christmas lunch and then slipping into a food-induced coma in front of the TV as we watch films all afternoon. I must have dozed off at one point as I wake to find my head on a pillow in Alex's lap, a blanket thrown across my body and his hand resting on my hip. I am so grateful for the return of this version of Alex that I lie there for a while, eyes closed despite being fully awake, savouring the moment.

# CHAPTER ELEVEN

I pull on my ball gown and then realise I have no way of zipping up the back. Try as I might, nothing is going to help me get that zip up. With a sigh of frustration, I realise that I am going to need Alex's help. I call down and moments later I hear his footsteps on the stairs. As he enters my room, I take in the sight of him suited and booted in his tux and, for a moment, my heart skips a beat.

I turn so that I am standing in front of the long mirror, holding up my strapless bodice, with my bare back to Alex. "Could you give me a hand with the zip? I just can't seem to get it to budge," I ask. Without a word, Alex crosses the room and comes to stand behind me. I catch his eye in the mirror and smile at him, but an expression I can't read crosses his face. I would say it was lust, but I know better than to think that Alex feels that way for me, no matter how tingly he makes me. His hand rests on the small of my back and I hear his breath hitch, but he doesn't say anything as he slowly, almost sensuously, pulls the zip up my back. Even when it is finally up, Alex doesn't step away. Instead, he rests his hands on my bare shoulders as he stares at my reflection in the mirror.

"You look stunning, Liv," he murmurs into my ear as his eyes run down the length of me in my midnight blue gown, and for a moment I wonder if he is going to kiss me. But then he shakes his head slightly as if to dispel a thought and instead holds up a red jewellers box. "I thought this would go with the dress," he says, opening the box and pulling out a stunning sapphire pendant set in platinum. He drapes it around my neck, fastening it at the back, and then stands back to admire it in my cleavage.

"Oh, wow. It's beautiful, Alex," I say, running my fingers over the cool stone. I think Alex is about to say something, but then he abruptly turns and stalks out the room with a strange expression on his face.

I add the final touches of my makeup and grab my clutch before heading downstairs to join Alex. Tonight is a huge New Year's Eve ball sponsored by Davenport Wines being held in Battersea Park and I know there are going to be a lot of important people there. I am kind of dreading it as there will be lots of schmoozing to be done, and inevitably I get left alone. All the wives seem to already be in their own cliques and I don't really fit in anywhere. But I will plaster on my smile because this is for Alex and I owe him for everything he has done for me.

The car ride is mercifully quick, and as we enter the marquee where the event is being held, I take in all the gowns surrounding me. Mine is positively dull in comparison, an intense midnight blue with a sprinkle of glittering sequins across the bust line, but when I went shopping, I wasn't really sure what would be appropriate. Alex keeps his arm around me the whole time we walk through the crowds greeting people, which is somewhat unusual, but whatever, I am just going with the flow.

Suddenly I feel him stiffen beside me and I look around for the source of his agitation, finally spotting a woman walking towards us in the most stunning crimson gown overlaid with black lace. Her raven black hair is pulled up and clipped off her face, accentuating her sharp features, and I sense purpose when I look into her icy blue eyes. Alex remains completely still as she approaches, and when I stare up at him, I notice the cold, hooded expression on his face.

"Alex, darling," the woman purrs, kissing him on both cheeks, before turning her eyes on me. "And this must be your lovely new bride," she continues, though her tone suggests that I am anything but lovely.

"Sofia," Alex acknowledges her. "Yes, this is my wife, Olivia. Olivia, this is Sofia Augustine, an old…business associate of mine." I smile politely at Sofia, but my subconscious is whispering, 'Business associate, my arse!'

"Pleased to meet you," I say, holding out a hand that Sofia ignores completely.

"Alex, we have not seen you at the club for a while now," she says, her voice low and probably meant for my husband's ears only, as she runs a scarlet painted nail down the sleeve of his jacket.

"I have been busy, Sofia," Alex responds brusquely. "Now, please excuse us. We have to circulate." Alex pulls me along before Sofia has a chance to respond, a little forcefully so that it makes it hard to keep up on my heels. I glance up at him and I can see Alex's jaw working furiously; I have never seen him quite this unsettled and my mind is racing as I try to figure out just what is going on.

Alex grabs a glass of champagne off one of the passing waiters and downs it in one gulp before requesting another and a soft drink for me. Well, at least he hasn't forgotten that I am here. "Are you okay, Alex?" I ask softly.

"Fine," he answers sharply, leaving me in no doubt that he doesn't want to talk about what just happened.

"Okay," I whisper, feeling like I have just been scolded.

Seeing my face, Alex's expression softens slightly and he suggests we make our way to our table for dinner. I nod my head and let him lead the way. It is only moments before I hear an announcement to sit down and soon people are following in our wake.

Our table is filled with the usual wine industry colleagues that Alex deals with, so I keep smiling and try to join in the conversation, but most of it goes over my head. After a while, I simply zone out as I try to puzzle through the incident with Sofia. The mention of 'club' is tickling my subconscious, but I just can't figure out why it is bothering me so much. I am lost in my inner musings when, suddenly, the hair on the back of my neck prickles, and when I glance around I see Sofia glaring daggers in my direction. The moment that she notices that I see her, her expression instantly smoothes into a neutral mask, and I start to wonder if I imagined it.

I barely manage to eat any of my dinner, delicious as it is, due to my stomach being full of nerves. Alex notices and I see the frown crossing his face. Not wanting to add to whatever is stressing him out, I deliberately pick up a forkful of chicken and stuff it in my mouth. I see his relief and I resolve to get through this evening with minimal fuss.

After dinner, there are a number of speeches and then a band comes on. The mixture of pop and rock has my feet tapping, and seeing this, Alex stands and asks me if I want to dance. I accept gratefully, anything to get away from Sofia's daggers, which continue to be sent my way when I am not looking directly at her. We spend the next few hours dancing away and I am grateful to see the tension no longer in Alex's face. We laugh as Alex tries to spin me to some fast fifties rockabilly number and it all goes horribly wrong when my feet get tangled in the long skirt of my dress. But fortunately he saves me before I hit the ground.

At last, some slower songs come on and Alex wraps me up in his arms and rests his chin on my head. As we sway, I listen to his heart thumping in his chest, trying to figure out the enigma that is Alex Davenport. Before I know it, the countdown to midnight begins and I grin as we shout along with everyone else.

As the clock strikes I turn to Alex, my breath catching in my throat. I know what is expected; we are husband and wife and everyone will expect a kiss. What I don't expect is for our kiss to spiral out of control as Alex is consumed by some unknown hunger, the same hunger I experienced briefly on our wedding day. He bites down on my bottom lip, causing me to yelp slightly, but all that does is give him access to explore my mouth. As his tongue clashes with mine, I find my whole body responding as I melt into Alex's hard frame. Alex's hands move down to cup my bum, kneading and grabbing hard enough to leave bruises, before one hand returns to grip the back of my neck tightly. Finally, Alex breaks away and we are both left breathless, staring at each other. My heart is pounding so hard in my chest that I am sure it must be audible to everyone around us.

"We're leaving," Alex states in a tone that brooks no argument. I merely nod in reply and let him lead me to the cloakroom to fetch my wrap, and then we are sitting in the car, being driven home. The tension between us is thick, yet neither of us has said a word. I glance up at Alex under my eyelashes and see his jaw clenched and an expression that I can't fathom in his eyes. Every fibre of my being is hyper-aware of Alex's masculinity, and a dull throb sits between my legs. I squirm in my seat, trying to find a little relief, when suddenly I am aware of Alex's scrutiny. His eyes bore through me, yet the expression on his face remains a neutral mask. A smirk appears as he runs his eyes over my body and I find my nipples hardening under my dress.

We have no sooner pulled up in front of the house than Alex is pulling me from the car and into the house. The door slams shut behind us and for a moment we both just look at each other, lost in the inevitable. And then Alex speaks. "Turn around, Olivia." The command is issued in a low, gravelly voice, completely at odds with Alex's regular teasing tone. The use of my full name startles me, and before I can think further, my body is already obeying. I stand still, my eyes staring up the stairs, as we stand in the frigid hallway, and I wait with bated breath. A few moments pass and all I can hear is our breathing.

Suddenly I am aware of Alex's arms coming over my shoulders and unhooking the cape at my throat. It slithers to the floor, and for a heartbeat, the world stops spinning on its axis. I shiver as I feel Alex's warm breath on my neck as, ever so slowly, he pulls down the zip of my gown. "Put your arms out and hold on to the end of the bannister," he instructs gruffly. I comply without rational thought, quietly awaiting his next command. The single movement has my dress pooling at my feet as I lean forward to grip the smooth wooden post. Large, agile hands skim down my sides until they rest on my hips and I am very much aware that my arse is now in the air, the angle of my body on my heels offering direct access to my damp, aching pussy. The hands follow a leisurely pace down the backs of my thighs and calves, until they reach my ankles. "Lift your foot and then the other," Alex orders. I comply and he pulls the dress out from around my feet, discarding it in a heap by the front door.

I glance back down at Alex, but immediately he notices. "Eyes forward," he barks, and I whip my head back around, my heart thumping in my ears. The cold of the hallway has raised goosebumps over my skin and I am shivering ever so slightly. I feel Alex stand behind me, heat radiating from his frame making the cold more tolerable, and then I hear him shedding his own clothes. My body is feeling ultra-sensitive, and the moment his hand snakes around my waist and deft fingers find my clit, I let out a low groan, as the warmth starts to spread across my pelvis. His pelvis pushes into my arse and I can feel the huge length of him grinding between my butt cheeks. Suddenly, Alex's other hand is grabbing my breast, pulling it from the confines of my strapless bra and, almost painfully, squeezing my nipple. Teeth nip at my ear and neck as he forces my head back, my back arching as I try to maintain my balance.

"I don't make love," Alex hisses into my ear. "I fuck, I root, I shag...but I don't do soft and I don't do sweet. Do you understand, Olivia?" I nod my head, a thousand conflicting thoughts swirling around my head. "If you want this to stop, you need to say so now..." he trails off and waits for my answer. My brain is telling me that this is all a bit weird, that this is not what I want, but my treacherous body has other ideas and so I keep silent.

"Fine," Alex growls as he steps back. My body is already missing his heat, but I don't dare look around to see where he has gone. I then hear the telltale sound of a condom wrapper and I realise that there is not going to be much in the way of foreplay. Then he is back behind me, gripping my hips tightly. I hear the rip as he tears through the silk of the French knickers I bought for our wedding day, and then he is sliding into my damp pussy. When he has filled me to the hilt, his hand snakes around again and starts playing with my clit, rubbing circles and pinching the tiny mass of nerves until I feel ready to explode. Just as I think I am going to tip over the edge, he whips his hand away. I let out a guttural moan, deep and low, in response, but then Alex begins to move inside of me. Small, sharp thrusts to start with morph into long, deep pushes that fill me to my core. I am still gripping onto the bannister post for dear life and I am sure that I will be leaving fingernail marks in the wood. A low, keening sound is coming out of my mouth as I feel my orgasm building once again. It builds and builds, my body feeling like molten fire, and I am not really sure how my legs are still supporting me. A hand grips my breast once again and I can feel my nipple being pinched hard. The pain sends sparks of electricity directly to my clit, and all at once, I am coming hard around Alex's engorged cock. My inner muscles grip him hard as the waves of my orgasm crash over me and I hear Alex grunting as he slams into me. With a final thrust he lets go, consumed by his own orgasm.

I don't know how long we stay like that, panting as we both try to get our breath back, but finally, I feel Alex's stance soften and then he is pulling gently out of me. "I'll be back in a moment, Liv," Alex murmurs and then he is gone. My wobbly legs finally give way and I find myself sliding down onto the cold tile of the entrance hall, still wearing my heels. My body is shaking, but I can't quite figure out if it is from the cold or the aftermath of my climax. Moments later Alex returns, carrying a soft blanket, which he drapes around my shivering frame. He is still gloriously naked and I take in the sight of the man in front of me. My mind is still fuzzy and I try to say something, but nothing comes out as Alex scoops me up as if I weigh nothing at all. I wrap my arms around his neck, resting my head on his shoulder as I close my eyes and he carries me up the stairs.

Gently, Alex lowers me onto a bed and I open my eyes to unfamiliar surroundings. I take in the masculine wooden furniture and dark blue cotton sheets and surmise that I must be in Alex's bedroom, the one room of the house I have never actually entered. My body is still trembling, despite the warmth of the blanket, so he pulls open the duvet, inserts me under it and then climbs in next to me, wrapping his body around mine.

We lie in silence for several minutes and I can hear his heart thumping in his chest. "You okay, Liv?" he asks softly. I try to wrap my brain around what just happened, but I think a part of me is in denial. This changes everything. How can we go back after this to the easy friendship that we had developed? There is so much to Alex that I just don't understand, starting with the basement and ending with that crazy voice he used while he was fucking me, and I just don't know what to think. And then here he is, after saying he doesn't do 'gentle', looking after me, holding me like I might break.

"I…I am fine, Alex," I whisper, but I know that I am lying. We have crossed an invisible boundary and I am aware that, at this moment, I have made the biggest mistake of my life…I have fallen in love with Alexander Davenport. I look up into his eyes and something tells me that Alex knows that I am lying, but he doesn't push it. A soft kiss lands on my hair, and fingers gently rub circles on my back. The warmth of the bed, coupled with Alex's soothing ministrations, soon has me feeling dozy. I long to ask Alex where we go from here, but instead keep my mouth shut and wait as sleep slowly descends.

I wake to the sound of a vacuum cleaner coming closer and closer. I am lying on my front, my arms hugging the pillow beneath me, as the events of the evening before slowly filter back. It suddenly occurs to me that I am not in my bed, so I stretch out my arm, only to find the sheets cool. I open my eyes, just as Alex's housekeeper, Mrs James, walks into the room. She is clearly startled to see me, and I find myself flushing with embarrassment that I have been caught in Alex's bed.

"Morning, Mrs Davenport," she says, clearly uncomfortable.

"Um, morning, Mrs James," I reply as I glance at the clock on the side. Heavens, I have completely slept through. "I am sorry. I didn't realise you were in today," I say.

"Not at all, Mrs Davenport, I wanted to stay on top of things," she responds, and I have to remind her, once again, to please call me Olivia. Mrs James has worked for Alex as his housekeeper for the last six years and comes in every day, apart from Sunday, for three hours. I have no idea what Alex told her about me, but she is obviously aware of our sleeping arrangements and our marriage. I have hardly seen her since I started living here, as she typically comes in for the morning after I have already left for work. But she keeps everything ticking over, ensuring that the pantry and freezer are always stocked and the house is always clean and tidy.

She backs out of the room, telling me that she will come back later. As soon as the door closes I jump out of Alex's bed wondering where the hell he is. I grab a dark grey robe that I notice hanging off the back of the door and wrap it around my frame. I poke my head out of the door, listening out, and when I hear the sound of vacuuming coming from downstairs I make a run for it, not stopping until I am up in my suite, the door closed fast behind me.

My phone buzzes on the side table where I left it last night, and when I check, I see an email from Alex. I hold my breath as I scan the few lines reminding me that he would be in Asia for the week and that we would talk when he returned. I have a vague recollection of him telling me about his early morning flight earlier in the week, but clearly it had slipped my mind.

I make my way into my bathroom and examine myself in the mirror. I don't look any different from usual, but inside I feel completely alien. I notice a mark on my neck, and when I examine it closely, I see that it is a bite. I don't even remember Alex biting me last night, but then I wasn't really aware of anything other than the feel of him fucking me. I run my mind back over the way he took command of me and try to understand why I just complied without a second thought. That voice, I think to myself. It is the only explanation. It was like, when he spoke, my body answered, no matter where my mind was.

I run myself a bath, my aching muscles having made themselves known, and sink into the hot bubbles as soon as the bath is ready. My mind continues to swirl and I find myself thinking back on the previous times that I have had sex. I have never been shy in bed, but my past relationships have always been a bit along the lines of wham-bam-thank-you-ma'am. Even Steve, my longest relationship, which lasted two years after university, had pretty much stuck to missionary position, apart from high days and holidays, when we might try something a bit different. Never in my life have I ever experienced the raw brutality of what happened last night. And as I find myself growing aroused by the memories, I realise that, actually, I loved it.

# CHAPTER TWELVE

I am sat cross-legged in the middle of the basement on the platform, which actually turns out to be a mattress on a solid platform, taking everything in. For the past week, curiosity has driven me down here each evening after work to try to work out what makes Alex tick. My Google history would make even the worldliest person blush, and my Amazon purchase history would rival that of a psychologist's. I think I am starting to understand Alex's world a little better, and now that I have explored his dungeon further with fresh eyes, I can actually see the purpose of most of the equipment lining the walls. I feel like I have become a walking, talking BDSM encyclopaedia, despite not having really experienced any of it for myself. Weirdly, my dreams have been growing darker and darker each night and twice now I have woken up from climaxing in my sleep. Never before has my little battery-operated boyfriend—or Bob, as I affectionately call it—had quite so much use.

Alex is due back tomorrow and I know we are going to have to talk. I have no idea how he feels about me, beyond the friendship we have forged, but I want to be able to tell him that he doesn't have to hide from me. The more I have read, the more I have come to the conclusion that Alex is a Dom, the dominant person in a consensual BDSM relationship. It seems that the voice he used would have been the one he has when he slips into his Dom role. The fact that I had never heard it until New Year's Eve is simply that he had never tried to dominate me.

I am still trying to get to grips with how a person

slips between the two personalities, especially as with Alex they seem so different, but I guess I will have to ask the question if I want answers. I pull out my notebook where, ever the researcher, I jot down my question so that I can remember it for later.

I am so engrossed that I don't hear the footsteps until I notice the shadow at the bottom of the stairs. I glance up and stare as Alex steps forward towards me, my breath catching in my throat, as I take in my first sight of him in a week. The first thing I think of, as I look him up and down, is that he looks tired. There are dark circles around his eyes and deep lines etched around his mouth.

"I thought for sure you wouldn't be here when I returned," Alex says flatly as he comes to stand in front of me. He runs his hand through his dishevelled hair, and when he takes in the sight of me with my laptop and notebook, confusion fills his features. "What are you doing down here?" he ask warily.

"Research," I say with a shy smile. "Why did you think I wouldn't be here?" I ask, and I know a puzzled expression must be on my face.

"Because of what I did to you. I bit you and fucked you like a piece of meat. Why on earth would you want to stay?" Alex is clearly agitated and I don't really understand what he is saying.

"So what?" I reply, not sure where this conversation is going.

"So you didn't ask for that." Alex lets out a deep sigh. "Liv, you deserve to be cherished and made love to. Not some mindless fuck in a cold hallway. I...I am just not capable of anything else," he continues sadly.

"What the fuck, Alex?" I ask. "For one, let me just

say that 'mindless fuck' was hot, like seriously awesome. And two, if I hadn't wanted it, I would have stopped you."

"No, you wouldn't," he replies quickly, and I look at him in surprise. "I have known since that first evening we had dinner together that you are a natural submissive and would respond to me with absolute compliance. I knew that if we ever got into...a situation...you would just go along with it."

"So you are saying I have no brain, no will of my own?" I reply angrily.

"N...no, that not what I am saying," Alex says, unsure of himself for the first time.

"Exactly. So I could have stopped you if I hadn't wanted it. But I didn't stop you because I was as aroused as you were. At that moment, it was like nothing else mattered. And what do you mean, you are not capable?" I ask, wondering where he was going with that.

Alex lets out another deep sigh before taking a seat next to me on the mattress. He stares resolutely ahead, not even looking at me when I nudge him with my elbow. Softly he begins to talk.

"I lost my virginity when I was fifteen to my high school girlfriend, Becca. We were in love—well, as much as you can be when you are a walking teenage boner. It was her first time too and I did my best to take it slowly, to make it romantic and gentle, but looking back it was like I felt numb. Even then, during the act, all I wanted to do was walk away. It did absolutely nothing for me. I should have ended it then, but this was Becca, the girl who had been my best friend since we were twelve, so we kind of just plodded along. Becca didn't realise how I was feeling, so she kept pushing for more sex and I kind of just gave in to it. But I was having all these fantasies about tying her up and smacking her arse till it was bright pink and I was completely frustrated because I didn't know how to deal with it.

In the end, I suggested trying something new and tied her up to a tree in the vineyard naked one day when I knew there wouldn't be anyone else around," continues Alex, letting out a mirthless laugh. "I blindfolded her and stepped away for a couple minutes tops to watch her reaction and she completely freaked out. Called me a pervert and all sorts of things, even though she had been up for it until that point. And that is how it ended. I knew there was something wrong with me, so I made a point of staying away from girls in general and only fucking the school sluts who were known for being easy when the need arose."

My heart breaks for the teenager that was Alex, in a tiny community where anything that was not the norm would be frowned upon. I wait as he carries on. "It wasn't until I was in my final year of uni over in Sydney, where I met Ronnie, that I really discovered who I was. She was five years older than me and into kink. We had an understanding; we were friends who fucked, but there were no feelings involved. She had just got out of a long-term relationship and I just didn't want the hassle of dealing with another Becca. We tried all sorts of things and would go to this club in the city. The day she asked me to beat her I nearly threw up. Needless to say, I didn't know what the hell I was doing and I hurt her, fractured a rib. Fortunately, she was the forgiving type and spoke to the owner of the club about mentoring me.

I was lucky. A couple of Doms agreed to take me under their wing and they guided me through the next couple of years. I soon learnt what got me off and I had a steady stream of willing subs who enjoyed that sort of thing." I raise my eyebrows as I wait for him to continue. "For me, I want complete submission. I am a sexual sadist who gets off on hitting willing women. I don't do intimacy. I can't. It is just not who I am."

It takes me a couple of minutes to process everything that Alex has told me and I am confused. "I don't get it," I say, and I feel Alex finally turn and look me in the eyes. "You say you don't do intimacy or gentle, yet you have been nothing but gentle with me. Yeah, I get that it doesn't arouse you, but you are not incapable, as you have just said." Alex goes to reply, but I continue on, "Okay, so what we did would not be classified by most people as 'making love', but afterwards you looked after me. You held me and made sure I was okay. If that's not intimacy, then I don't know what is."

Alex stays quiet for a moment, processing my words. "But I was rough, and I bit you, for Christ sakes…"

"And I enjoyed it," I interrupt. "Are you telling me that your subs don't get off on that sort of thing?"

"Yes, but there are contracts, limits, safewords…" Alex trails off.

"Okay, but essentially this was the same, just with nothing formal. If I had said stop at any time, would you have?" I ask.

"Of course!" Alex exclaims loudly. His body is like a tightly coiled spring, just waiting to erupt.

"So what's the problem then?" I ask.

"How the hell do you know about any of this?" Alex suddenly asks, his eyes narrowing as he contemplates me.

I feel a blush spreading across my cheeks. "Um, I spent the last week researching pretty much everything about BDSM," I say quietly. "I wanted to understand you. I wanted to understand my reaction to you."

"And what reaction was that?" Alex asks, and at last I see a little of his trademark smirk falling back into place.

"When you told me what you wanted me to do in your Domly voice, it was like nothing else mattered. Every thought went out the window and my body just responded like it knew I could trust that you would take care of me…and you did," I say.

"Domly voice?" Alex asks, looking a little perplexed.

"Yup," I say, letting out a small breath. "Completely different from your normal voice. I noticed you used a little of it when we met at the auction, but I guess I didn't get the full shebang until New Year's," I joke, trying to lift the mood.

"I wasn't aware I had a voice," Alex responds. "So this research…how does it make you feel about all of this?" he says, sweeping an arm around the room.

"Nervous," I say. "But a little excited too. I…I never knew that sex could be so carnal, and there was part of me that fucking loved it. Reading up on the psychology behind it all was really interesting, and I could pretty much pass a test if it came to naming everything on that wall," I say, gesturing to the racks of canes, whips and other restraints. "But it is all a bit in the abstract, you know. I read a couple of BDSM novels and they aroused me, but I don't really know what exactly it was that aroused me." I glance up at Alex, suddenly feeling shy in my confession, and I see something in his eyes that instantly makes me wet.

"Then let's find out, shall we?" Oh my, the Domly voice is back. Alex stands and takes a step back and I see that his posture has changed as well.

"Stand up, Olivia," Alex orders, and I find myself complying without a second thought. "Take your clothes off, fold them neatly and leave them in a pile on the couch. Then I want you to return to this spot and face that wall," he says, indicating to the wall across the room.

I do as I am told and moments later I am standing naked next to the platform, facing the far wall. I notice that my laptop and notebook have been removed and that a pair of leather cuffs is now lying on the cover. My breathing quickens and I can already feel the dampness between my legs as I watch Alex stride over to a rack and pick up a flogger. He runs his finger through the tails while he contemplates his choice. He goes to find a crop as well, before returning to me. I know my eyes must be the size of saucers, but I sense that he is building the anticipation.

"Lie down on the mattress on your front, arms above your head, resting your cheek on the cover," Alex says. I do exactly as he asks and he strides around the platform confidently to where my wrists are. He quickly cuffs them before attaching them to a rope that comes out the side of the platform so that I can't move my arms. Alex then moves behind me and I can see out of the corner of my eye that he now has a further two cuffs, which he attaches around each ankle and then secures them so that my legs are spread. I can feel the cool air between my thighs and I find myself squirming in expectancy.

A moment later Alex comes around and kneels in front of me, his eyes hard. "Choose a safeword," he says. "Make sure it is something you can bring to mind readily."

"Daisy," I whisper, as my favourite flower springs to mind.

"Be aware that I am going to test your limits, so screaming, crying out 'no' or 'stop' won't do anything. But if you really want this to stop, say 'daisy', and it will be over in an instant. Okay?"

"Okay," I respond, knowing that I am about to walk into the unknown.

"Promise me!" Alex stresses, and I catch a glimpse of the soft side he seems to think he doesn't possess.

"I promise," I respond clearly.

Satisfied, Alex nods his head. "I am going to blindfold you now," he says just before slipping the cloth over my eyes. Instantly I am in pitch black and my other senses are on high alert. I hear Alex moving about the room, and that only furthers the anticipation. Suddenly I hear music, some kind of soft drumming that seems to match the rhythm of my heartbeat. It is a little louder now, but I can still hear Alex's movements.

I wait and I wait and then I feel it. The soft tails of the flogger caressing my skin as it makes a path down my neck, across my back and then across my butt cheeks. My nipples are erect, burning even, in my arousal and I can feel the dull throb in my pussy. The flogger continues its journey across my body and down my legs before returning upwards. I gasp as I feel it getting higher and higher, and then it is right in the apex of my thighs, running across my sensitive clit. I moan as the throb turns to shooting sparks of pleasure in my abdomen.

Then suddenly the flogger is gone. I wait a moment and then feel as it comes down on my bare behind. I am anticipating a stinging sensation, but instead I hear a light thud and all I feel is warmth spreading across the area where Alex has struck me. Then the flogger is back, running its tails across my skin before coming down on me, slightly harder this time. Alex repeats this action several times in time to the drumming, making my heart beat faster each time I anticipate a strike.

I am startled when I hear something drop on the floor and then I feel Alex shift me. Suddenly I feel two fingers thrust into my wet, needy pussy and I let out a low moan. "Someone is enjoying this," Alex states. "And you taste so fucking good. I think it is time to take this up a notch."

My mind is racing, and as I remember the crop, I find myself tensing, slightly scared about what's to come. Without warning, I hear a whoosh and then my arse is on fire as the crop connects with my already sensitive skin. I scream out in response, already tensing for the next strike, when I feel Alex's cool hand running over my hot skin. "Fucking beautiful," I hear him murmur before planting a kiss on my behind. He moves away and I brace myself for the next hit. When it arrives, it is painful, but now that I know what I am expecting it is less scary. Alex repeats his soothing action with his cool hand and his kiss, and I finally start to relax when I realise that it is not going to get any more painful than this. Alex starts to work a pattern on my behind, but I am hardly aware of it as my mind seems to slip away, lost in the sensations and the drumbeat.

The throb between my legs is desperate and I am completely consumed by my need for release. I am vaguely aware of the crop hitting the floor and my ankles being released before I am being flipped over. The sheets are cold and fresh on my painful behind, bringing relief to my overheated skin. The mattress dips and I feel Alex between my thighs, a pillow being slid under my hips. And then he is inside of me and I cry out in relief. A hand comes down and pinches my clit and I shatter as my orgasm consumes me. The hard thrusts continue and the angle of Alex's cock makes the pressure on my G-spot unbearable. Just as I catch my breath, I feel the tightening of my pelvis once again, the sparks in my abdomen and then I am falling apart, ripped to shreds. Alex never stops his relentless thrusts as I come over and over around him, calling out that I can't take anymore. Finally, I hear him grunt as he finds his own release and I feel his body collapse onto mine.

I am still floating away, detached from my body, my mind still trying to comprehend the mass of sensations I have just been subjected to, when I feel Alex move off me. With great tenderness, he removes my blindfold and releases my wrists, rubbing them to bring back the blood supply. I am vaguely aware of him disposing of the condom and then bringing out a soft blanket and a couple more pillows from the chest of drawers. He slips a pillow under my head, settles the blanket over me and then climbs in beside me. He pulls me into his embrace, gently kissing my hair as he runs his fingers over my body.

I slowly come back to myself in Alex's arms, and I find myself staring up at him in wonder. "That was…" I whisper, trying to find the words. "That was phenomenal. I never knew I could feel like that," I say. Suddenly unsure, I need to know if it was good for him as well. "Was that okay for you? Did it get you off?" I ask, a little afraid that maybe I am not enough for him.

"Oh, Liv, that was spectacular, baby. You did so well. To answer your question, yes, it was good for me. It was actually fan-fucking-tastic," Alex responds, smiling down on me.

"Oh, good," I murmur. I reach up with my hand and cup Alex's cheek, stroking his jaw with my thumb as I look deeply into his eyes. I do the one thing that I have been craving since the clock struck midnight on New Year's and bring his lips down to mine. The kiss starts off slow, but when I feel a small bit of resistance on Alex's part, I open my eyes to see the battle raging inside of him. He wants this tenderness, but some part of his brain is telling him he is not capable, and so he is fighting it. I do my best to ignore the war and focus on moving my lips against his. I pour my feelings for Alex into the kiss, and finally, I feel him start to respond. He nips my lower lip and I open my mouth to give him access.

I don't know how long we make out for, but eventually the evening's activities take their toll and I feel my eyelids growing heavy. Sensing my tiredness, Alex breaks the kiss and rolls me over so that he is spooning me, his warmth enveloping me. We really should go upstairs, but I guess neither one of us wants to move. I feel Alex moving his hand around the edge of the bed and I vaguely wonder what on earth he is doing until the lights go out.

"Doesn't do intimacy, my arse," I say softly, and I feel Alex smile into my hair before planting a soft kiss on my head.

"Sweet dreams, Liv" is the last thing I hear before exhaustion claims me.

# CHAPTER THIRTEEN

A week has passed since our night in Alex's dungeon and I have not laid eyes on him during that time. That's not to say we haven't communicated; I have had plenty of emails, text messages and even bunches of flowers. Yet every night I fall asleep alone in my own bed, and wake up alone, the only sign that Alex has even been home being the dent in the pillow next to mine and the smell of him on my sheets. I am so frustrated I want to scream.

I am pottering around in the kitchen after a long day at work, making myself a cup of tea, when I hear the front door slam so hard I swear the hinges rattled. I make my way through to the entrance hall and look around, wondering what the hell is going on. I spy Alex's coat flung on the rack, and I cast my eye around looking for clues. I hear more thuds and, as I spot the open door to the basement, a ginormous crash. I am apprehensive now. This is completely at odds with Alex's normal calm and collected behaviour, so I creep down the stairs as quietly as possible, wondering what I am going to discover.

I cast my eye around the room as my feet hit the final stair, and all I can see is carnage. A chest of drawers has been flung over, the mattress is lying half off the podium and I can see that a rack of equipment has been torn off the walls. Alex is pacing like a caged animal, and in the low light, I can see the tension radiating off his taut frame. I watch as Alex mutters to himself, stoking the rage inside of him until finally he turns and puts his fist through one of the walls. I flinch and draw back up the stairs as I contemplate what I need to do.

My mind is swirling and suddenly seizes on a piece of information sitting in my subconscious. In all our conversations this week the one thing that really stuck in my mind was Alex's need for control, which was not something I had ever really noticed about him. I think back and recall the email he sent:

*Liv,*
*You ask me why I go to The Club...Well, why do people join gyms? Why do people join tennis clubs and so forth? I guess the first answer is to be around like-minded people. But I guess, for me, it is my way of centering myself. Some people do yoga; I spank some woman's arse. No matter what is going on in my life, whether it is business or personal, I can deal with it when I am going to The Club regularly. It is really only there that I can find the peace, the calm even, that I need to function.*
*I don't know if that makes any sense to you.*
*Alex*

In an instant, I know what I need to do. I may not know the cause of Alex's anger, but I think I have a way of calming him down. Before I can think too much about what I am about to do, I quietly slip out of my clothes. Naked as the day I was born, I make my way back down the stairs as silently as possible. I pause for a moment at the bottom, steeling myself for the unknown that I am about to encounter. With Alex's back turned towards me, I slip silently into the centre of the room. I kneel down on my haunches, tucking my feet under my bum, spreading my legs out like I had read about. I bow my head and rest my upturned hands on my thighs. My body is shaking; the adrenaline and nerves threaten to overpower me, but I am determined to do my best. To be the perfect little submissive.

I stay as unmoving as I possibly can, willing my limbs to still as I wait for Alex to notice my presence, keeping watch for his reaction from underneath my lashes. After what feels like ages, Alex finally whips his head around and sees me. His eyes grow wide, and for the first time since I have been watching him, his agitated body quietens.

"What the hell are you doing, Liv?" Alex hisses.

It takes a moment for me to think of the words I need to say. "You look agitated, sir. I thought perhaps I could be of assistance?" I am hoping I have struck the right balance of submissiveness. The moment 'sir' passes my lips, however, I notice Alex's body language shift; already the tension is leaving him and he seems looser somehow. His eyes have become hooded and I can see the vein in his neck pulsing.

"Oh, you did, did you?" The Domly tone has returned and, weirdly, I feel myself becoming wet with his words. "Well then, be a good little sub and get yourself over there." Alex points at what I now know to be a whipping bench and I feel myself growing cold with fear. Mutely, I comply and I wait for further instructions. "Bend over the bench and put your arms in front of you."

I do as I am told and wait as Alex cuffs my wrists and secures them to the bench. Despite the padding, my knees grind into the base, making me feel uncomfortable—though I guess that is probably the whole purpose—, in addition to how exposed I am currently feeling with my arse in the air. I watch as Alex regards the floor strewn with equipment. His face is calm and neutral and I haven't got a clue as to what he is thinking. My heart sinks when I see him finally bend down and pick up the one thing I was truly dreading: a cane.

Just the thought of what Alex is going to do with it has my body trembling. He sees my reaction and a look of triumph stretches across his features. Oh-so slowly, Alex walks towards me as he weighs the cane in his hand, occasionally bringing it down on his palm with a soft tap. The anticipation is killing me, and not in a good way either.

He moves behind me, but I don't dare turn my head to see where he is. Yet my senses are on high alert, telling me that he is only a couple of feet away. I hear the sound of shoes being kicked off, and in my mind's eye, I see him rolling up the sleeves of his shirt. Then he is back and I can finally see him out of the corner of my eye. I see him balancing the cane in his hands once more, twirling it in his deft fingers, like it is a maker of magic rather than the monster I think it is.

I close my eyes, trying to blot out my fear. Moments later, I hear a woosh as the cane slices through the air and my buttocks explode as the slice of pain sears across my skin. It lingers, a sharp, stinging sensation that fades only slightly into a dull burn. "Count it out with me!" commands Alex, and I yell out "One" through gritted teeth, loathe to give him the satisfaction of seeing me cry.

Without warning, the second blow falls and reflexively I cry out "Two!" This time, however, tears have formed in the corner of my eyes and I feel one slide down my cheek. I have no idea how many strikes he is planning on giving me and this unknown variable makes the anticipation even worse. I know for a fact that I am going to have some serious bruises in the morning. A third falls and I scream in response, my arse raw and on fire. Somehow, I sense he is taking care to not hit me on the same spot twice, but it doesn't make a difference to the pain that is now all-consuming.

Two more rain down on me and I am sobbing uncontrollably. My whole body is shaking and somewhere in the back of my mind it occurs to me that I could use my safeword. The word 'daisy' flickers in my mind's eye like a neon sign, but I know deep down that I won't call it out. Something is driving my need to prove to Alex that I can take whatever he wants to dish out, and I am not sure it is healthy for me, but I am going to do it anyway.

"Five more," Alex grunts through gritted teeth and I can hear him breathing heavily, though I am unsure whether it is due to arousal or exertion. I don't say anything in response and simply wait for the sixth to fall. I notice this time that, despite the pain it still inflicts, there was less power behind the strike. My sobbing continues, despite my best efforts to rein in my emotions, as another two strikes fall, each slightly lighter than the last. By the time the tenth comes down, it is barely a tap on my ravaged skin and I cannot think straight through the agony. My sobs have changed to a strange keening noise that sounds alien even to my ears.

"Oh fuck! What the fuck have I done?" I hear Alex mutter to himself, his tone empty and desolate, as he steps away from me, before the world suddenly goes black.

*~*~*~*

I claw my way out of the blackness to find that I am lying on my front, in a bed. Instantly I know that I am not in my bed by the scents that tease my senses; I am in Alex's gigantic bed. The coolness around me tells me that I am alone and I spend a moment mentally checking on my body. My bottom smarts, but I know nothing is broken so I crack open an eyelid. I cast my eyes around the room, using the moonlight filtering through the curtains to guide them until they come to rest on Alex, sitting across from me in an armchair. His trousers are rumpled and he has stripped off the shirt he was wearing earlier, leaving him in only a white singlet. He is watching me intently, a look of abject sadness on his face.

"Hey," I whisper. "Are you okay?"

"She asks if I am okay..." Alex mutters, as if he is talking to someone. "What the hell?"

"Alex, seriously, are you okay?" I repeat, wincing as I roll over onto my back and sit up. In an instant, Alex is by my side, trying to support me. I bat his hands away, grimacing with irritation. "I am fine, Alex. Really!"

"Oh, Liv, what the hell have I done?" Alex asks, resting his forehead against mine.

I reach up my hand and cup Alex's face, staring up into his troubled eyes. "Oh, Alex," I sigh. "Stop this. I am not broken. My arse might feel like it is on fire, but no harm done," I say, attempting some humour to try to lighten the situation. I can feel that we are both walking an emotional tightrope and one wrong move might send either of us spiralling into oblivion.

"Liv. Oh, Liv," Alex says, his voice hollow. "I could have really hurt you, you know. I wanted to..." he trails off.

"But you didn't," I soothe, running my fingers across the soft bristles of his day-old stubble. "What happened? What set you off? I have never seen you like that," I say.

Alex sighs and, at that moment, looks completely broken. He runs his hand through his hair and pinches the bridge of his nose as if he is steeling himself to deliver bad news. "I have spent the whole of the last week, since our night together, trying to understand why the hell you seem to want me. Each night I would come into your room and lie beside you as you slept, beating myself up for corrupting you. This beautiful angel who is nothing but kind and compassionate to everyone she meets and I have utterly defiled and marked her." I go to interrupt, but Alex holds up his hand, so I stay silent. "I tried to come up with every reason to make you leave, to persuade you that I am no good for you, but every fibre of my being was telling me that I wanted you to stay. I realised that I had fallen in love with you and probably had been for a while." I gasp softly at his words but let Alex continue. We'll definitely be returning to the whole 'love' thing.

"This morning I had made up my mind that tonight I was going to come home and tell you how I felt, ask you to give me a chance..." he trails off.

"So what happened?" I ask gently.

"Your father turned up at my office today," Alex states flatly, his eyes filled with a grief that I don't understand.

"What the hell?" I gasp. What on earth does my dad have to do with any of this? I haven't seen him since I was thirteen. "I...I don't understand..."

"Well, it seems like your father has not been as

absent as you thought. He has been keeping tabs on you since your mom threw him out, and then when you and I got together…" The expression on Alex's face tells me that he is wrestling with some inner demon.

"Just tell me, please, Alex," I plead. My heart is hammering in my chest and a pit of dread seems to have opened up in my stomach.

"Goddamn. That piece of shit came into my office today to blackmail me, Liv. Somehow he knew everything about me, even had some rather explicit photos of me at The Club. He threatened to leak them if I didn't pay him a hundred thousand pounds." I leap out of the bed and start pacing agitatedly as I try to take in everything he is telling me. "And then here's the kicker, Liv. If this had been about you and your well-being, then I could have totally understood a protectiveness on his part, but the fucker…" I hear the break in his voice. "The fucker didn't even ask about you. He just wanted the money."

I don't even realise that I am crying until Alex is moving across to me and enveloping me in his arms. "I…I am so sorry, Alex," I sob. "This is all my fault."

"What the hell, Liv?" Alex hooks a finger under my chin and forces me to look up at him. "How is any of this your fault?" he asks, a serious expression on his face.

"He's my father," I say simply, between my sobs. Before I can say anything further, Alex scoops me up and returns us both to the bed. Settling with his back to the padded headboard, Alex cradles me in his arms, tucking the duvet around us both. He waits for my crying to cease, all the while murmuring soft reassurances in my ear.

The tears finally abate and a question suddenly pops into my head. "How does he have pictures of you?"

A hard look crosses Alex's face and his jaw tightens. "I have an idea, but I need to check a few things out before I know for sure. Cameras aren't allowed in the club." Alex swallows hard. "I need to check with the club records to work out exactly when they were, but I think they were just before Christmas."

"What are we going to do?" I whisper, staring up into Alex's troubled eyes.

"We are not going to do anything." Alex stresses the word 'we' and I find myself instantly shaking my head knowing that I can't leave him to sort out my mess. "I am going to handle this, Liv. There is no need for you to get involved," Alex says in a vain attempt to reassure me.

"But I can't let him do this. You have worked so hard to keep this under wraps, and then I come into your life and everything is ruined." I feel dreadful and have no idea how to fix this situation.

"Stop that," Alex commands. And the Domly tone is back. "Nothing is ruined. I will handle this."

I nod and squirm in Alex's lap. That voice seems to have the power to make me wet instantly. "Alex?" I say.

"Yes, Liv?" Alex responds gently.

"Did it help?" I ask, trying to hide the tremor in my voice. "I thought…"

Alex lets out a deep sigh and I know he understands what I am asking. "No, Liv, it didn't. For a few minutes, I felt centred again, calm and collected like it normally would make me feel, but when you started crying for real there was none of the excitement, none of the arousal I would usually feel. Instead, I just felt hollow and empty, and terrified that you would hate me."

I can see the pain in Alex's eyes and I would do anything to take it away. "Oh man, you mean I sacrificed my arse for nothing?" I joke weakly, trying to elicit a smile.

"Oh, Liv, baby, how can you joke about what I just did? I mean, you should probably be pressing charges..." I watch as Alex trails off, his devastation at what has just occurred written all over him.

"Alex, listen to me. What happened was consensual. I knew what I was doing when I walked into that room. I understood the risks. I might not have enjoyed it, and quite frankly that kind of pain does nothing for me, but that wasn't the point. I wanted to do that for you. And anyway, I had my safeword. If I had really needed to, I would have used it."

"Oh, baby," Alex says, cupping my face. "My brave, brave girl," he murmurs before bending his head down and brushing my lips softly with his. "I think you deserve some extra-special TLC." I am suddenly very aware of my naked state as I lie in Alex's lap. The hand cupping my face slowly makes its way down my neck before settling on my breasts. With the lightest of touches, Alex begins teasing my nipples, swirling his fingers over the sensitive nubs and adding light pinches.

Warmth spreads across my skin and the throb between my thighs intensifies. Alex begins to nuzzle my ear and neck, teasing my lobe with his teeth. I close my eyes, the sensations overwhelming me. "Open your eyes, Olivia," Alex commands, and instantly they snap open in response.

Just when I don't think I can take anymore, the hand caressing my breasts slips down between my thighs. His fingers trail lightly across my sensitized skin, goosebumps rising in their wake as they slowly move higher and higher. I am aching for Alex's touch, and when he finally slips between my wet folds and draws a finger across my swollen clit, the sparks of arousal that are shooting through my pelvis ignite into wildfire. I gasp and Alex increases the pressure on my sensitive nub.

I am so lost in the sensations that I am barely aware of Alex propping my torso up on some pillows so that he can use his other hand. Suddenly, I feel a couple of fingers slip inside my drenched pussy. As Alex moves them around he finds that secret spot buried inside of me. My hips arch up as I come with a load moan, my inner muscles clenching around the fingers pumping into me. All the while Alex never lets up the pressure on my clit. Like a master, he draws out my orgasm so that by the time the last wave subsides I am spent and breathless. I am coming down from my high when I feel Alex shifting out from underneath me, laying me down gently before coming to kneel between my spread legs. "Is this okay, Liv?" I hear Alex ask softly. I nod, the need to have him inside of me becoming intense.

"Alex, please, I want to feel you…I am on the pill…" I plead.

"Are you sure, baby? Just so you know, I have never gone without a condom."

I nod and reach out for him.

The sensation of Alex pushing into me is agonizing in its slowness. When I am full to the hilt, I hook my ankles behind Alex's knees, pulling him deeper than I thought was even possible. Alex comes down to rest on his elbows, his hands tangling in my hair, as he slowly starts to kiss me. The action of his tongue mirrors that of his cock as he slowly thrusts into me. The fire inside of me is raging once again as each stroke takes me higher and higher. When, at last, I am not sure that I can take anymore, I explode. My body shudders and trembles around Alex. "Open your eyes, Olivia." Once again I obey Alex without thought. Watching Alex's face as he continues to thrust into me is the most erotic thing I have ever seen, and in response I feel my pelvis tightening, the tell-tale signs of my imminent climax. With a final thrust, Alex is consumed by his own orgasm, his frame stiffening above me as he spurts into me hard and hot, setting off another wave of pleasure that rocks me to my core.

I am slowly coming down from the overwhelming sensations still washing over me when I feel Alex shift off me. Moments later, Alex returns with a warm cloth and proceeds to clean me up with the utmost tenderness before climbing back in beside me and pulling me into his arms.

"I thought you didn't do vanilla," I whisper, a smile stretching across my face.

"Only for you, Liv. Only for you," Alex responds, his voice hoarse and low, but I can hear the softness coming through.

# CHAPTER FOURTEEN

Daylight streams through the cracks in the curtains, waking me from my deep sleep. I shift and can feel the stiffness radiating through my body. Somehow in my post-orgasmic bliss, I managed to forget about my bruised arse, but as I roll over, I let out a small yelp.

"Liv?"

I turn my head to find Alex regarding me with sleep-filled eyes.

"Sore arse," I murmur.

"Roll on your front," Alex commands, and I comply immediately. He slips the duvet down to reveal my bottom lined with red marks and faint bruising. "Fuck, Liv, you have no idea how horny it makes me seeing you like this." He runs a light hand over my sensitive cheeks. "Oh, baby," he says in a worshipful whisper. With gentle hands, he moves my knees, pushing them underneath me so that my arse is in the air and I am balancing on my elbows. Before I can think about what he is doing, Alex starts by laying a trail of light kisses all over my skin. I shiver, the sensation sublime, as my body responds to the gentlest of caresses. The kisses turn to licks and then Alex is running his tongue down the seam between my cheeks, over the delicate rosette of my butt. I tense and try to wriggle away, the sensation feeling entirely wrong.

"Stay still, Olivia!" The command is accompanied by a light tap on my hip, and quickly I fall still. I breathe deeply, trying to overcome the discomfort I am feeling in this new situation. "Good girl. Now relax." A hand snakes around my hip and the fingers focus on my clit, swirling and pinching, as I gradually grow breathless under Alex's attention. Completely distracted, I am only vaguely aware of another finger swirling around the entrance, until suddenly I feel a pushing sensation in my bum. Immediately I freeze, my breaths coming out short and shallow, in response to the intrusion. "Relax, Olivia. I am not going to hurt you." My body immediately responds to the tone in Alex's voice, and I find myself automatically letting out a deep breath and unclenching my muscles. Alex pushes his finger further and all at once I am full, but full in a weird, dark way that I would never have anticipated. "That's it, baby. Just breathe." That, coupled with the non-stop attention that my clit has been receiving, means that I know that my orgasm is not far off.

"Fuck, I can't wait," Alex mutters. I feel the head of his cock at my entrance and then he is pushing deep inside of me. The finger in my arse starts swirling gently, eliciting an intensely erotic sensation that I am not prepared for while Alex stays still, buried inside me. "You are so tight, baby. Fuck, I don't know if I can hold back."

"Then don't," I growl through gritted teeth, as I become needy for my orgasm. My body is prickled in sweat as every nerve ending is overstimulated. Slowly Alex draws out both his cock and finger before slamming back into me. My back arches and my fingers clutch desperately at the sheets as I explode, my orgasm all the more intense with his cock at this angle. Alex continues his thrusts, his fingers still buried in my arse and pinching my clit, and my next orgasm hits me with the force of a freight train. I cry out loudly, the words incoherent.

"That's it, baby. I wanna hear you fucking scream my name. I own your orgasms…this is all mine." At his words, I come again violently, my body shaking fiercely, every nerve in my body on fire. And then Alex is spilling his seed into me, his thrusts never abating until I come for the final time, shouting out his name. My body is shaking and tears are leaking out my eyes with intenseness of what I have just experienced as Alex gently pulls out of me. My mind is elsewhere, though, lost in the supernova that has overtaken me. Seconds later, he is cleaning me up once again, before pulling me into his arms and covering us with the duvet.

I lie limply in Alex's arms, waiting for my body to calm as he smoothes the hair back off my face. The expression in his eyes is calm yet I sense emotion rippling through him. Before I have a chance to say anything, a loud beeping noise interrupts us. It takes me a second to realise that it is actually the alarm on my phone, and as I glance around, locating it on the nightstand, I realise Alex must have brought it up with him last night.

"Shit, I'd better get up; otherwise I'll be late for work." I sigh and stretch my arms out above my head.

"You are not going anywhere today, Liv," Alex grumbles, burying his head in my neck and kissing the sensitive skin behind my ear lightly. "You can play hookey for one day."

I scrabble for the phone, finally turning off the incessant beep. "Alex…" I wheedle. "I can't just skive off." Truthfully I would rather stay here in bed with Alex all day, but if I don't work, I don't get paid.

"Is Charles in the country?" Alex's voice is mock-stern and I can't help but let out a small giggle.

"No," I reply.

"And do you have a deadline?" he asks, his expression deadpan.

"Nope," I respond with a roll of my eyes.

"Well then, one day won't matter," Alex says earnestly. "Besides, I need to spend the day with you. It's been too long since we just hung out, you know. And…" Alex suddenly looks a little embarrassed as he trails off.

"And what?" I ask curiously.

"And I miss my best friend." Wow, Alex just told me that I am his best friend and my heart is doing somersaults.

"Well, if you put it that way…." I smirk at him, quickly tapping out an email to let Charles know that I won't make it into the office. "So what does this make us then? Friends with benefits, or something?"

"Or something," Alex says quietly. We are both lying on our sides facing each other, and I sense there is something he wants to say. "Liv, I meant what I said last night about loving you. I am not exactly sure when you crept into my heart, but all I know is that the thought of you leaving, it just kills me."

"Alex, you have my heart too," I say. "Truthfully, I think I knew it when you kissed me on our wedding day. I love you and have been convinced that you didn't feel the same way. I knew we were friends and I loved that, but a part of me has always wanted more."

"Liv, I have a confession to make." Alex suddenly looks uncomfortable and I wait as it takes him a moment to continue. "That day at the auction I was going to beat you no matter what the cost." I must look as puzzled as I feel as he carries on, "I had seen you quite a few times at the auction house before. I would watch how serious and sad you were, as if you had the weight of the world on your shoulders, and how focused you were on making sure you won your lot. You intrigued me and I found myself wanting to protect you, even though I didn't have a clue what from. I watched your body language and knew you were a submissive, even if you didn't know it yet. And it spoke to me, drove me crazy until I did some research. I found out all about you and your mother, and I knew if I waited, an opportunity would present itself. I was terrified about revealing myself; I thought there was no way you would be into the lifestyle, so I was determined that I would be there for you no matter what, even if it meant that we would only be friends. And then there you were that day, so desperate and I was so cold, but you were so brave. Somehow, everything fell into place, whether it was luck or whatever…"

Alex is watching me warily and I guess he is waiting for me to be angry, but actually I don't care how orchestrated our meeting was because, at that point, I was at rock bottom and didn't have a clue how to drag myself out of the mess that was my life. Instead, Alex had taken me under his wing and nurtured me, and here I am in his bed while he tells me he loves me.

I reach out my hand and pull his head down to mine in a soft kiss before looking deep into his eyes. "I don't care about the past, Alex. All I care about is the here and now." Alex pulls me into a fierce hug and we stay that way for several minutes as he strokes my back, until Alex insists on running me a bath.

The water is blissful as I settle into the bubbles.

My eyes are closed as I float in the claw-foot tub, my mind relaxed and clear. I hear the door open and soft feet pad in. Opening my eyes, I spot a completely naked Alex holding out a mug of tea for me. I take in the taut planes of his body, the defined muscles that come courtesy of his morning gym visits, the slim hips and, eventually, his eye-wateringly large cock. Even in a semi-aroused state it is still magnificent, standing proudly to attention, and I find myself licking my lips nervously at the thought of something so big inside of me. Finally, I look up into his face, his day-old stubble a contrast to his normal pretty-boy surfer-dude looks. The twinkle in his eye lets me know that I have been caught out ogling him.

"I hope you didn't give Mrs James a fright, wandering around the kitchen like that," I say, only half-joking. I take a sip of the steaming brew before setting it down on a small cabinet to cool down properly.

"Nah, I gave her the day off. Texted her earlier." Alex gives me a smirk, leaving me in no doubt why he wants the house free of interruptions. "Scoot over," he instructs, before climbing in opposite me, the water splashing over the edges as he makes himself comfortable. We soak in silence for several minutes and just enjoy the quiet. My mind is busy, though, trying to work through everything.

"Alex, my dad…" I begin, the nerves starting to ripple through my stomach.

"Liv, we are not talking about that today. Today is all about pleasure…nothing is going to spoil it."

"Oh, okay," I say, my body shivering slightly at the use of the word 'pleasure'. Alex picks up one of my feet and starts kneading it, digging his knuckles deep into the arch. The feeling is divine and I close my eyes, lost in the sensation of having my foot massaged. It is not long before he swaps feet and goes to work on the other one. I let out a moan of appreciation and I feel his cock twitching against my calf.

I am barely paying attention until, suddenly, I feel Alex's hand at the apex of my thighs. My eyes fly open as I feel Alex pushing down on my clit with his thumb. The pressure is constant, yet he doesn't move, instead concentrating on the foot he still has in his other hand. A dull ache begins to grow in my groin and I find myself wanting to move, to gain some friction against the sensitive little nub. My body attempts to buck of its own accord, but the rest of Alex's hand is holding my pelvis down firmly, and I find myself immobile. I stare at Alex's face, the naked arousal evident in his expression. Maintaining eye contact with me, his brings his mouth down over my big toe. He nips the end and I feel a jolt of electricity directly in my pussy. The pressure on my clit steadily increases as Alex begins to suck and nibble my toe. Oh fuck, whoever thought toes could be erotic?

The ache in my pelvis turns into an all-consuming throb, as I feel the blood rushing in my ears. Only then does Alex start to move his thumb in very deliberate circles. My body is insatiable in its responsiveness and I throw my head back over the edge of the tub as I quietly beg for more. I am rewarded by Alex moving his hand round to push two long fingers deep into my slit, all the while never ceasing his thumb movements or the sucking of my toe. How the hell is he this dexterous? With a slow deliberateness Alex begins to fuck me with his fingers, drawing them all the way out before plunging them back in.

"Alex," I whimper, my body completely overwhelmed yet still pleading for more.

"Do you want it faster, baby?" Alex asks, his voice thick with arousal. It is all I can do to nod and all at once he starts driving into me in short, sharp thrusts. My muscles tighten around Alex's fingers as my body starts to tingle. A coolness seems to seep up from the toe that is currently being suckled upon and my body starts to shake as I near my climax. I am gripping onto the edges of the bath tightly, my back arching out of the water as my pussy greedily begs Alex for more. I am so close to coming when I feel Alex withdraw his fingers completely. I whimper with dissatisfaction until I feel the hard pinch on my clit. The searing pain immediately turns to a white-hot burn and that is all it takes for me to explode, my body going completely rigid as my climax drives electricity into every nerve ending. In my haze, I am aware of Alex plunging his fingers back inside of me, his relentless pace drawing out my orgasm almost painfully while I plead for him to stop and to give me some relief.

"No way, baby," I hear him chuckle. "Come for me one last time, Liv." His words send the world spiralling and then I am weightless, adrift in a sea of sensation. I go completely limp, and in the abstract, I am vaguely aware of Alex moving my body around so that I am now leaning with my back against his chest. I slowly come back to myself with my cheek pressed into the smattering of soft hair on Alex's chest. His hands never stop moving across my body in long, languid strokes as he plants small kisses over my hair.

"Mmm, um, wow," I mumble and I feel the rumble of Alex's laugh through his chest. We lie like that for several minutes until I am aware of something very hard poking me in the back. I reach my arm back, sliding it between our bodies and wrap my hand around the end of Alex's swollen cock. I let my fingers play with the end, drawing back its hood and teasing the slit. I hear Alex catch his breath, and a smile plays on my lips with the knowledge that I can elicit a response like that out of him.

I suddenly feel Alex move from behind me. I turn my head, thinking he is about to get out of the tub, that maybe he doesn't like what I am doing, but instead I see him settle his backside on the rim of the bath. I swivel around on my haunches so that I am facing him, and when I look up at him, I see the desire in Alex's eyes. His beautiful pink cock is right in front of my mouth and I lick my lips like this is the tastiest morsel that I will ever put in my mouth. Slowly I slide my mouth over his head. The skin is silky and slick under my tongue and I am gratified when I hear a low moan coming from Alex. Using my fingers to pull back Alex's foreskin, I begin by swirling my tongue around the exposed head and slit.

I feel Alex slide his fingers into my hair, gripping my head tightly. A slight pressure lets me know that Alex is taking over control. I can think of nothing else apart from pleasing him and allow him to push further into my mouth until I can feel him at the back of my throat. I can feel my gag reflex kicking in and my body tenses. Immediately Alex withdraws slightly, whispering, "Relax, baby." I respond by running my tongue over the length of him. I start a slow sucking motion, hollowing out my cheeks, and Alex responds by controlling my head in a gentle bobbing rhythm. The bath is a bit slippery, so I reach my arms around his hips and hold on to his arse cheeks. I can feel the muscles in his thighs rippling as he fights for control, but I know from the twitching I feel in my mouth that he is not far off. I bring one hand back between his legs to find his perineum. I start with slow, firm strokes, but when I hear his raspy rumble, I stroke with greater pressure.

"Fuck, I need to be inside of you, baby," Alex gasps, suddenly pulling out of my mouth. In one fluid motion, he slides back down into the tub before bringing me down directly on his engorged cock. I am so turned on and wet that I slide down on him easily, my tissues stretching and accepting his enormous length eagerly. Slowly I start to move again, using my knees to bring me up before allowing gravity to pull me down again. Alex reaches between us and slides his fingers across my clit, all the while staring deeply into my eyes. Need for friction drives us both faster and faster, until at last, I feel Alex rippling under me. I watch as he clenches his jaw, his orgasm rocketing through him, yet not once does he close his eyes, his intense stare searing through me. The hot spurt of his cum finishes me and I climax with him, my back arching at an impossible angle while my inner muscles convulse around his cock. When we are both spent, I collapse forward onto Alex's chest and he brings his arms around me, soothing me with gentle words.

The water has cooled and I start to shiver, so Alex hauls us both out the tub and into the shower. The cubicle is soon full of steam and the jets get to work on muscles that have been used more in the last twenty-four hours than in the last decade. Alex grins at me as he lathers up some delicious smelling shower gel in his hands before smoothing them gently across my weary body. I lean against the wall as Alex washes me thoroughly, even bending down to part my swollen sex lips and giving them a once-over. He soaps up his own body and then pulls me into his embrace under the shower head, his lips brushing mine lightly, as the cascade of water rinses us.

If I was ever in doubt of Alex's feelings for me, then that kiss would be the thing to dispel them. Tenderness washes through me as we make out for what feels like forever. Eventually, the water runs cool and we both jump apart. We step out of the cubicle giggling and moments later Alex wraps a gigantic warm towel around my frame before slinging one around his hips. I realise that I have nothing down here and let Alex know that I need to go upstairs to my suite to get dressed. He nods and, surprisingly, follows me up the stairs.

I make my way through the small living area towards my bedroom, which has its own walk-in wardrobe. Alex follows me, flinging himself on my bed and watching my movements wordlessly, whilst I go through my meagre collection of clothes, looking for something comfy to wear.

"Liv?" Alex asks softly. "Is that all you got in there?" he says, gesturing to the small rack of dresses that I bought for his functions.

Suddenly I feel really embarrassed that he has caught me out. Despite Alex's very generous monthly deposits into the bank account that he set up for me, I never felt that I could spend the money on something as frivolous as clothes. Instead, I had set up standing orders for several charities that I feel strongly about, and the rest is just sitting there, adding up. Now that I no longer had the expense of my mother's care hanging over me, the money I earned from my job was enough for me to buy clothes for work and a few luxuries, as well as being able to put some extra aside. The rest of the time I lounged in years-old broken-in jeans and long-sleeved T-shirts.

"Um, yeah," I respond as Alex stalks into the closet, opening drawers and examining the contents.

"Liv, you deserve to be dressed like a princess," Alex says earnestly.

I shrug at this strange statement. Suddenly he is pulling me into his arms and staring down on me intently. "You are mine, Liv, and everything of mine is yours. You deserve to be spoilt and pampered, yet you take nothing."

"Oh, Alex, I don't need clothes," I say. He picks up an old cardigan that I use for mooching at home in and holds it up, examining the holes in the sleeves with an arch of his eyebrow. I snatch it off him, exclaiming, "I don't go out in that. Besides, it was my mother's."

"Whatever, Liv. I think we need to take you shopping." I studiously ignore him, hoping that he will drop the subject. I pick out a pair of functional cotton panties and a matching bra, before pulling on a pair of soft black jeans, a long white shirt and a thin canary-yellow cardigan, gifts that Alex gave me at Christmas. Today I feel like dressing for him. Going back out into the bedroom, I sit at the table, where I rough-dry my hair and add a touch of makeup. Not once do Alex's eyes leave me, and he has a strange look on his face.

I am just turning my head round to smile at Alex

when my stomach lets out the most almighty grumble. I giggle and Alex lets out a loud chuckle. "Right, time for some food. Let's go out," Alex suggests, and I smile in agreement. "Meet you downstairs in five," Alex says before heading back to his own room to get dressed.

*~*~*~*

We are sitting in Bluebird on the King's Road, just around the corner from the house. Breakfast has been ordered and I am sipping on a cup of tea gratefully, having never actually gotten around to drinking the one Alex brought me in the bath. Away from the house and Alex's 'distractions', my head is bursting with questions. I think it is the researcher part of me that means I am never fully satisfied until I have covered all my bases.

Alex sits back, appraising me. "Talk to me, Liv. What's going through that mind of yours? I can see the cogs turning."

I stare at the table, picking at the serviette, knowing that I might be opening a whole can of worms that I shouldn't. I take a deep breath. "Alex, what happens now? I mean, you have subs, don't you? I guess what I'm trying to say is, where the hell do I fit in this?"

"Look at me, Liv," Alex instructs, and I tear my eyes off the table. "Okay, firstly I don't really have a sub." My eyebrows raise but leave him to continue. "What I mean is there are a lot of Dominant/submissive couples that only play together, regardless of whether they are a couple in real life. Do you understand what I mean?" I nod in response. "At The Club, there are a number of subs who are happy to play with a variety of Doms. I travel so much that it has never appealed to me to have my own sub. Instead, I would see who was available, and if they wanted to play, then we would.

"At The Club, every person, Dom or sub, has a profile written about them detailing preferences, limits and so forth, so you get an idea of who you are compatible with. Plus the owner makes it his business to ensure that everyone is matched up correctly. It is all safe, sane and consensual, you get me?" I nod again, doing my best to absorb everything he is telling me. "Over the years, I have gotten to know the subs, and in turn they have gotten to know me. I have a couple of favourites who enjoy the kind of pain I dish out, but there is no exclusivity or anything, and I certainly don't have any relationship with them outside the scene."

"Oh," I say softly. I can see from the openness in Alex's expression that he is telling me the truth. "I didn't like it!" I blurt out suddenly. "The caning. It was too much and I know that I could never do it again." I feel a shudder run through my body at the memories flooding through me. "I did it because I wanted to help you, but I know that I am not strong enough to do it again." I realise that I am babbling and take a deep breath and close my eyes, forcing myself to calm down.

I feel a hand envelop mine on the table and I open my eyes to find myself looking into Alex's eyes, eyes that are filled with compassion. "Oh, Liv, I would never, ever do anything to you that you did not want. Do you understand?" Tears fill my eyes and I bob my head in response.

"But I will never be enough for you if I can't give you that," I say sadly, the thought that has been buried deep in my subconscious finally coming to the surface.

"Oh, Liv," Alex says, running a hand through his tousled hair. "Liv, listen to me. I am going to be completely honest with you. I have been to The Club exactly twice since we got back from Australia. The first time was after you discovered the playroom and seemed so disgusted with me. I needed to reaffirm with myself everything I believed to be true. The second time was last week."

My heart sinks at the thought of Alex having sex with someone else after my experience with the flogger. My horror must show in my face because Alex quickly clarifies, "Nothing happened, Liv. I was so confused about my feelings towards you that I just needed to escape and find a bit of serenity. When I got there, Jessica, who has always been one of my favourites, approached me to do a scene. I had her tied to a St Andrew's cross, her arse all rosy, but all I could see was you in my head. After a couple minutes, I knew I couldn't go through with it and had to hand Jessica off to one of the other Doms. That's when I knew…" I hold my breath as I wait a beat for him to continue. "Knew that you were it for me."

My tears are openly falling down my face, my hand gripping tightly onto Alex's. "I am as unsure as you where we go from here, but I can tell you this. For the first time in my life, vanilla sex was fucking awesome." His words make me giggle and I swipe away the tears with my napkin, his revelation filling my heart with hope. "For so long, love and sex had to be separate in my life, Liv. The only way sex could satisfy was if it was brutal. Yet here I am, wanting to make love to you over and over, like a man in the desert longs for a drink of water."

The waiter approaches with our food and we break apart with a smile. I glance down at my eggs royale and realise that I am ravenous. Alex reads my thoughts and smirks at me as I dig in like it is my last meal ever. The eggs have been poached to perfection and the hollandaise sauce makes my mouth water. Alex attacks his own full English with equal vigour and for a while there is silence as we savour our food.

When every morsel has been cleared and Alex declares himself stuffed, we resume our conversation. "Alex, just so you know, if you need to go to The Club because you need it, please just tell me, okay? I couldn't bear it if we had secrets like that between us."

"Liv, your trust in me is the most precious thing in the world. I would never, ever do anything to abuse that, you hear?" I nod as I see the truth shining out of his eyes.

"Also…" I take a gulp before I speak, my words hardly above a whisper, "I don't think I could ever be a slave. I started reading about that and, argh, that is so not my thing!" I see Alex holding in a laugh.

"It's not mine either, Liv. I have no desire to dominate you in real life. You have seen where I come from…Do you think any female I grew up with would have allowed me to tell them what to do?" I think of the forces of nature that are Alex's mother and his sister, Nadia, and I find myself grinning. "No, for me, it is purely sexual," he says. "Look, I think maybe we both need to sit down and work out some guidelines so we can find the parameters we are both comfortable with." I raise an eyebrow in response, a million questions running through my mind.

"Like, for example, if you are agreeable, then in the playroom I would like you to submit to me fully, call me sir…" Oh my, I think to myself, as a delicious heat starts pooling between my thighs. "But in the bedroom, that's just Alex and Liv. What do you think about that?"

"Is that why you only call me Olivia when we are in the playroom?" I ask the question that has been burning inside of me for some time. I have always found it a little strange that the only time Alex ever calls me by my full name is when he is in full-on Dom mode.

"Hmm, I have never really thought about that but, yeah, I guess it helps me to separate things in my mind," Alex says.

My cheeks are flushed and I can see Alex appraising my body language knowingly, a sexy smirk on his face. I nod and duck my face down, feeling shy all of a sudden. A finger hooks under my chin and once again I am looking into Alex's smouldering eyes. "Liv," he says softly, "your submission is the greatest gift you could ever give me, and believe me when I say that I will treasure it always." I gulp down a breath, suddenly feeling light-headed and starved of oxygen.

"Oh, Liv, this is just the beginning…"

# CHAPTER FIFTEEN

I lean my head against the cold window of the train carriage and sigh. I am exhausted. It has been two days since I got the call from Charles that interrupted my brunch with Alex and I was forced to cut our day short. Charles had received a call about one of the most challenging books we have been trying to trace. A private collector in France was offering it up for purchase and so, of course, Charles expected me to go at the drop of a hat, even though I was supposedly 'sick'.

So here I am, after an excruciating forty-eight hours, returning empty-handed to a furious Charles. It's not my fault that the manuscript was a fake, a very good one at that, which is why it took me ages to verify, but that doesn't stop Charles from behaving like a brat when things don't go his way. It didn't help either that the owner of the document was indignant when I told him that it was a forgery and threw me out of his house, calling me a liar and a charlatan. At least that's what I understood from my school-time French. I rub my forehead, trying to ease the tension headache that I feel forming behind my eyes, as I wait for the Eurostar to pull into St Pancras International so that I can go home, get into a nice hot bath and maybe have hot sex with my husband. It is Saturday after all.

Finally, the train pulls into the station and I am grabbing my small case off the shelf before that train has even ground to a halt. As I step off, I glance around to find the exit when I suddenly hear my name being called. My head whips around to find

Alex, leaning against a railing casually, looking disturbingly handsome in his long black coat and the grey scarf I gave him for Christmas. Before I know it, my feet are carrying me towards him and I fling myself into his open arms, nuzzling into his chest. I feel safe. I feel like I am home. Alex's strong arms envelop me and I feel his fingers running through my hair. "I have missed you, Liv," Alex murmurs into my hair, before tilting my chin up and bringing his mouth down onto mine in the sweetest of kisses.

I break off the kiss so that I can look Alex in the eye. "I missed you too, Alex. What are you doing here anyway? I was going to grab a taxi."

"I didn't want to wait. Besides I have good news, so we are celebrating," he tells me, picking up by the waist and swinging me around as if I weigh nothing, causing me to break out into a fit of giggles. Before I can say anything else, Alex grabs my hand and leads me across to the champagne bar and snags us a couple of seats on a banquette. As I sink down onto the leather, I feel a pleasant warmth beneath my bum and realise that the seats are, in fact, heated. Lovely!

"So what are we celebrating?" I ask, curiosity getting the better of me.

"I'll tell you in a moment. But first things first..." Alex trails off before ordering a bottle of the Krug Grande Cuvée Brut, from the waitress who appears instantly at the touch of a button. Yes, they actually have a 'Press for Champagne' button which makes me smirk. I study the beautiful vaulted ceiling and the art deco lamps that create a lovely ambiance in what is actually a bustling train station while we wait.

"So here's the thing," Alex starts, his voice low. "I met with your father today." Instantly my spine stiffens but I wait for him in silence to continue. "Since his visit to my office, I have had a private investigator digging into his past and it turned up some really interesting things."

"Like?" I ask, my curiosity piqued.

"Like the fact that he has actually been in the States for the last ten years and only moved back to the UK a few months ago, to escape some major charges of fraud. When I confronted him about that, he freely admitted that he had lied and had not actually been keeping tabs on you. The first he knew about us was when he received an anonymous package with the pictures, along with info about our wedding that my sister posted on Facebook. I get the feeling that whoever took those pictures is looking to get to me and probably did some digging on you and found the perfect target."

"So what does all this mean?" I ask, hesitant about how much I really want to know.

"Well, I did some bargaining of my own. Told your father that if he handed over the pictures then I wouldn't go to the US authorities and let them know where he is. He seemed quite happy with that deal," Alex finishes off sarcastically.

"That's one problem solved but it still doesn't solve the issue of there being pictures in the first place." Alex's expression darkens for a moment at my words but clears as the waitress brings the bottle of champagne along with a couple of glasses.

"I think we need to celebrate. The rest is being looked into but tonight we can toast that we have at least won the battle," Alex says, pouring out the champagne in both glasses.

"Um, Alex, I think you are forgetting something. I

don't drink," I say softly.

"Liv, it is time to put this in the past. Your father is out of your life and you don't ever have to worry about him again. I would never let him anywhere near you. I am not asking you to drink the whole bottle. Just have a taste and see if you can work your way past the fear."

I know it is completely irrational to have held on to this for all this time, but I have only to think back to that night, and him screaming in my face, to smell the wine fumes that make my stomach roll. I steel myself knowing that it is time to pull on my big-girl panties. As the Aussies would say, 'Suck it up, princess'.

"Okay, just a sip. But if I don't like it, then…" I trail off, not wanting to hurt Alex's feelings.

"Then nothing. I am never going to force you to do anything you don't want, Liv. I promise. But it is not in my nature to not challenge you and push your boundaries," he adds with a knowing smirk. I hold up my champagne glass and move it forward to touch Alex's with the softest of 'clinks'. I take a tiny sip, waiting for the taste in my mouth to trigger the usual awful memories. But instead all I experience is the fizz of the bubbles with a zesty lemon note.

"Mmm," I say, savouring the flavour.

"Mmm good?" Alex asks, his brow arching and lips twitching in a barely suppressed smile.

"Delicious," I say, taking a bigger sip this time.

"Well then, only the finest champagne in the future for you, Liv," Alex retorts with a laugh.

I take it slowly, knowing that I am not used to drinking, but even so, by the time the glass is half empty, I can definitely feel its effects. I am giggly and flirty and I can see that Alex definitely has a twinkle in his eye as my hand brushes across his cock through his dark grey jeans accidentally.

"Come on, let's get out of here," Alex says, glancing at his watch. "Time to take you shopping like we were supposed to the other day before your boss so rudely interrupted your day of skiving off."

"Alex, you've got to be kidding," I say. "Let's just go home. I feel grotty from the train and need a bath."

"I have plans for you, Liv. And I have an appointment arranged for you, so we are going. Or do I have to spank your arse?" Oh my, that tone makes me instantly wet, and I can feel the flush rising up my neck. I nod my acquiescence and let him lead me out of the station and into a taxi where he murmurs our location to the driver, too low for me to hear. The journey whizzes by. The sexual tension rolling off of Alex is palpable, making me somewhat nervous. He is constantly touching me, running his long fingers over my jean-clad legs and burying them in my crazy hair. At one point, he leans in to suckle my neck, and damn it if the arousal inside me doesn't become an all-out burning inferno.

Before I know it, we are pulling outside a small black storefront and I look up to see 'Agent Provocateur' written in a gorgeous pink script. Lingerie. Okay, I can do this. I take Alex's hand as he leads me into the shop and I am astonished when the assistant walks over and greets him by name. Clearly he has been here before. A streak of jealousy runs through me as I think about all the other girls he may have been buying underwear for and I don't even realise that I am scowling until Alex chuckles next to me. "Liv, I can read you like a book. There is nothing to be jealous about. I was in here yesterday organising this for you," Alex whispers into my ear, and I immediately feel myself relax.

The assistant now introduces herself to me as Tammy and requests that I go on through to the dressing room. I follow her through the store, eying up the beautiful confections of lace lining the walls, sure that my expression probably speaks a thousand words, as she leads me into what feels like a sumptuously decorated boudoir. With a brisk efficiency that immediately puts me at ease, Tammy asks me to strip down to my bra and panties so that she can size me and then closes the curtain behind her. I shrug out of my heavy coat and peel off my jeans, and moments later I am standing in front of a full-length mirror, casting a critical eye over my body.

I am not skinny by any means; since being with Alex, I have filled out rather a lot but mostly in the right places. I suck in my stomach trying to erase the tiny little bump that I see there. But otherwise I am just an ordinary girl: average height, average build and pretty average boobs. What Alex sees in me is still beyond my comprehension.

Tammy calls out to ask if I am ready, and when I reply to the affirmative, the curtain whips open and then is closed again briskly behind her. In the briefest of moments, I spot Alex smirking at me through the gap before Tammy ensures that the divide is properly shut. She eyes me for a second before asking me to turn around and then bustling back out again. She is back moments later with a handful of bras, which we then spend what feels like an age trying on. At first I feel so embarrassed about having her hands on me and I apologise profusely when she looks at my old greying cotton bra, which she tells me is really the wrong size.

When I finally turn around and look at myself in the mirror, I actually gape at my reflection. The black bra that Tammy has put on me is underwired with a full cup, but the lace work is stunning. Somehow the shape has given my breasts an incredible lift and it has transformed how my entire body looks. Oh my god, I never knew a bra could change my appearance.

"Wow," I say softly to Tammy.

"I know, right?" she responds with a kind smile.

"So how much is it?" I ask nervously, trying to calculate if I can afford one or two of these beautiful creations.

"Um," Tammy says, looking at me. "Mr Davenport bought a whole lot of the collection for you already." I gasp and she looks at me quizzically. "Did he not tell you?" she asks, her voice now a quiet whisper.

"Nope," I sigh quietly. Seriously, what is this man thinking?

"Oh okay. I am just measuring you to make sure that we send across the right sizes."

"How much?" I ask, and I can see her nervousness at the brusque note in my tone.

"Um, about ten thousand," Tammy responds.

"Ten thousand!" I screech, before flinging the curtain open and marching up to Alex, the fact that I am wearing only a bra and panties completely forgotten. "What the hell, Alex? You could fucking feed a village in Africa for that. I don't need ten thousand pounds worth of bras and panties. Are you friggin' crazy?" I am breathing heavily, rant over, when I remember my near-naked state. I quickly fold my arms across my body defensively as I wait for Alex to answer me.

Taking my arm firmly, Alex guides me back into the changing room before turning to me and looking me straight in the eye. "I spent ten thousand because I wanted to, Liv. You deserve the best. And you will accept the underwear. Otherwise, I am going to have to show you what happens when you disobey me." Yeah right, so much for him not wanting to dominate me outside the bedroom! His tone is silken, but I feel the steely resolve in his words and his eyes are intense as they bore into me. Alex has backed me up against the wall, his frame becoming the prevailing feature in the small room. My breath hitches as he brings up a hand and runs a finger lightly across the lace on the top of my breasts. Instantly my nipples harden beneath the soft tulle lining and I feel wetness spreading in my panties.

"Fuck, Liv. You look like a peach, all ripe and soft, waiting to be bitten." I can feel teeth scraping my ear lobe as he murmurs the words so quietly that only I can hear him. I am so completely distracted by his words that I don't even realise that his fingers have slid into my panties until I feel them slide in between my wet folds and then into my slit. The heel of his hand grinds against my throbbing clit as he starts to pump his fingers into me. Immediately my muscles clench around him and I can feel my breathing becoming ragged. Seriously, this man unravels all my control and turns me to putty with his touch.

"Alex," I whisper hoarsely. "There are people outside."

"Then you are just going to have to be quiet, my

love. You need to learn what happens when you pick battles over something so silly. I always get my way, one way or another."

I moan softly as Alex brushes that sweet spot buried deep in my core, causing sparks of electricity to start firing through every nerve ending. In my effort to be silent I can feel every muscle in my body becoming rigid, and my hands claw the walls.

"That's it, Olivia. Give it up to me, baby. I know you want to. Come for me." His final command, combined with the teeth sinking into my neck, has white-hot light shooting through my core as I convulse around Alex's fingers. When I finally stop trembling, Alex removes his hand and brings his fingers up to his mouth, very deliberately licking each one clean as he watches me. "Fuck me, you taste good," Alex murmurs when he is finished, before planting a soft kiss on my forehead. And then, with a wicked gleam in his eye, he turns and stalks out of the changing room and I hear him talking to Tammy on the other side of the long velvet curtains.

With trembling hands, I remove the bra and put my old one back on before pulling on my jeans and buttoning up my white shirt. I look at my reflection in the mirror and my eyes seem wild. I take in the sight of the livid mark on my neck where Alex bit me and, weirdly, I don't feel revolted. Quite the opposite, in fact. Seeing Alex's mark on me makes me feel cherished almost, and more than a little horny. Knowing that I don't have time for the self-analysis, I take a deep breath and pull on my coat and scarf, grateful for the camouflage that they afford.

As I pull the curtain aside and step forward, Alex is instantly by my side, his large hand folding mine.

"You are not going to argue with me now, Liv, are you?" he asks. I shake my head in response, unable to formulate any words in my current state. Several bags are waiting on the countertop and Tammy lets us know that the rest will be delivered. She gives me a knowing look and I can't help the blush that creeps up my face. I have just climaxed in a public changing room, for heaven's sake. As Alex turns around to gather up the bags, Tammy gives me a quick wink and a smile; I know immediately that she is not judging me and I find myself relaxing slightly. Smiling back, I thank her for her help before Alex escorts me from the store.

As we step outside into the cold winter air, I ask Alex quietly if we can go home; I just want to go somewhere private to regroup. We are still trailing around my small case and are now laden with the bags, so Alex hails another taxi and it is not long before we are pulling up in front of the house. I have just stripped off my coat and am hanging it on a peg when Alex turns me gently to face him. "What's the matter, Liv? You are really quiet."

I shake my head. "Nothing's the matter, Alex," I say quietly. "I am just trying to process, that's all."

"Process what?" Alex asks, narrowing his eyes as if he is trying to see right into my soul.

I offer up a small smile. "Well, the fact that I just came in a public place. And...and you bit me."

Alex's face darkens as he pulls aside my scarf gently, scanning my neck for the marks that he has left. I can see anger rippling under the surface. "Shit, Liv, I didn't even realise. Fuck, I am so sorry, baby."

I put a finger up to his lips and he looks at me in surprise. "Don't be sorry," I say, and his eyes widen.

"I liked it. I am just trying to process why I liked it. It's not something I ever thought I would be into, but…" I trail off feeling embarrassed and turn my face to look at the floor.

"But what?" Alex says, hooking a finger under my chin and forcing my head up to meet his intense scrutiny.

"But when I looked at myself in the mirror and I saw that you had marked me…I felt…I felt cherished. I don't understand it…it just doesn't make sense to me. And it made me horny, which just seems weird."

"No weirder than how horny it is making me right now, looking at my mark on you," Alex says, fire in his eyes. "I will always cherish you, Liv. With every breath that I take." With that, he brings his mouth down onto mine in a hunger-filled kiss, his tongue fucking my mouth with deep, deliberate strokes. Without breaking off for breath, he scoops me into his arms and carries me through to the living room, where he deposits me on the long grey sofa. Our hands are a tangle of limbs as we try to strip each other of our clothes.

When we are finally naked, Alex settles between my legs, resting on his elbows, but makes no move to enter me. I am wet and pulsing, but when I tilt my hips towards his pelvis he shakes his head. "Not yet, Liv. I want to worship this amazing body of yours." His voice is filled with lust and heat and I find myself squirming in anticipation.

With the slowness that only a man in complete control could exhort, Alex trails his hands down my body, closely followed by his mouth. Caress. Lick. Kiss. And so it goes until he has covered every inch of my front. My fingers have wound into his hair and find myself pulling on it each time he finds a particularly sensitive spot. Eventually, he returns and captures a nipple in his mouth, whilst he rolls the other sensitive nub between his fingers. Instantly, the electricity that I felt earlier begins its path to my core, lighting up nerve endings as it surges through me. I groan under his ministrations, the ache in my pussy becoming an all-encompassing need.

"Please, Alex, I need you. In me," I gasp.

"All in good time, baby," he mutters, before biting down on my nipple and pinching the other. And just like that my orgasm crashes over me. Holy shit, I never knew I could come just from having my nipples played with. Before I have even begun to come down from my orgasm, Alex has buried his head between my legs and is running his tongue over my clit. The stimulation is too much and I come again hard, wave after wave annihilating me until my body is rigid and arched clean off the couch. Yet Alex never ceases his relentless attention. Instead, his arms curl up underneath me, supporting my frame and holding my bucking hips still.

I cry out Alex's name over and over as the heat blinds me. I can feel tears running down my face and I am not sure how much more I can take. Just when I think I am actually about to break with the intensity of the fire inside me, I feel Alex shift, and then he is sliding his cock deep into my pussy. "Fuck me, Alex. Please," I scream, needing to feel him move inside of me.

"Okay, baby," he grunts as he starts slamming into me, his fingers expertly moving across my clit. Alex is so deep it is almost painful, but the ache soon blossoms into a tsunami of pleasure that engulfs me. I am vaguely aware of Alex coming, his hot seed spurting into me with his own release, and then I am climaxing, my overwrought body finding a final release of its own.

I come back to myself to find Alex's head resting on my chest, his body draped over mine, panting as if we had just run the hundred meters. I move my fingers across his back in slow circles, enjoying the feel of him beneath my fingertips for a change. Slowly, he lifts his head and gives me a lazy smile. "You okay, Liv?" he asks softly.

"All good, Alex," I whisper. In seconds, Alex is off me and I am cradled in his arms like a baby. I am so completely drained as he strokes my hair and my face, whispering how much he loves me, that I find my eyes closing as the exhaustion consumes me.

# CHAPTER SIXTEEN

I am hot and sweaty, the beat of the music an additional heartbeat thumping through my body. I can feel Alex grinding into my arse behind me to the sexy Latin beats, his hands holding on to my hips firmly, as I lean into his body. We are in Floridita, a Latin American-inspired restaurant with live music in the heart of London's Soho, and for the first time in my life, I don't feel completely awkward in a club like this. It is so far from my usual scene—aka staying at home and reading a book—that usually the idea of getting dressed up and going clubbing like a twenty-year-old would fill me with dread. But instead tonight I feel a little like Cinderella, transported into an alternate universe.

When I woke up from my nap earlier to find myself still cradled in Alex's arms, it felt like I had slept for hours despite it only being around thirty minutes. I felt completely renewed, so when Alex suggested going out I had agreed without hesitation. "I want to take you out dancing," he had said, and even though it wasn't exactly my cup of tea, I had remembered how much fun we had at the ball, so I had smiled and said okay.

It had taken me ages to figure out what to wear, not least because, in the two days that I had been gone, all my possessions had been brought down into his room and put away in his massive closet. I had been touched to find that he had even included things like the quilt my mother and I pieced together as a project while I was at school, which I found neatly folded over the end of Alex's bed. Our bed, I need to keep reminding myself.

In the end, I had settled on a little black wrap dress in silk that I have had forever. It is sleeveless, with a sash that ties up at the waist and falls to just above my knee. I teamed it with a pair of Louboutin knockoffs that I found in Camden market—gorgeous booties with sheer lace over the top of my foot with a lovely floral detail. But the real surprise is underneath. Alex had been in the shower when I had gone through the packages we brought home earlier in the day. When I saw the set, I immediately knew why Alex had chosen them. The bra, thong and suspenders are all made of soft hand-woven elastic in a combination of thin and wide straps that criss-cross my skin in a cage-like pattern. When I had finally got everything on and fastened my stockings, I had just enough warning of the shower turning off to quickly slip on my dress and heels. The last item that had gone on was a thick metallic bronze choker collar. I had tried to hide Alex's bite mark with makeup to no avail, and there was no way I could just leave it as it was, so I was glad to find the collar when digging through a box of old jewellery. The heat in Alex's eyes and his straining erection when he emerged from the bathroom were all the confirmation I needed to know that I had made the right choice.

The first hour in the club we dance non-stop. I wouldn't have a clue how to salsa, yet my body seems to tune into Alex's and before long I find a rhythm that doesn't make me seem like an ice-skating giraffe. Instead, in Alex's arms I feel sultry and sexy. I feel Alex's hand roaming all over my body and then sense him stiffen slightly. "Are you wearing what I think you might be?" he whispers into my ear, his arousal evident in the hoarseness of his voice.

"Uh-huh," I respond, and I can feel his mighty erection digging into my hip.

"Fuck this, Liv. We are going home now!" Alex orders. I think about arguing and playing games, but I know that Alex will win one way or another and I am not ready to make an exhibition of myself in the middle of the dance floor.

"Okay." I shrug and give him an innocent smile.

"Naughty girl," he murmurs into my ear, as he practically drags me out onto the street and into the first available taxi.

The journey is mercifully short and it seems like only minutes before we are standing in the hallway, looking at each other. I notice Alex taking a deep breath before looking at me straight in the eye. "Do you want to play, Olivia?" Domly Alex asks, tilting his head towards the basement door.

My nipples instantly harden and my thong is wet with my arousal at his words. I am a little nervous about going back down there after last time, but I trust Alex and this is what this is all about. Submitting to him and trusting him to push my boundaries. I nod. "Say it, Olivia," Alex commands.

"Yes, sir. I want to play," I respond, slipping into the role.

"Very well. I want you to go down the stairs. Take your dress and choker off and kneel at the bottom. Keep everything else on." His voice is warm and deep, stoking something inside of me. A little devil, I think, just waiting to hear her master's voice.

"Yes, sir." I slowly walk down the stairs, not wanting to trip. When I reach the bottom, I quickly untie the sash and remove the dress, folding it neatly and placing it on the stair. I sink down onto my knees, adjusting myself to keep the heels from digging into my bum. It's only once I am in position that I look up and out into the room in front of me.

The lighting is dim, but I immediately see the changes that have occurred since the last time I was down here. The deep crimson walls are gone and instead they are dark purple fading into a dark inky blue. Tiny LED lights are dotted everywhere, giving the impression of the night sky. The raised bed in the middle is now covered in a cream faux-fur throw along with a stack of cushions in grey, purple and black, in all different textures. The 'furniture', as I have come to think of the equipment, is all there, bar the whipping bench, but it has been shuffled around a bit. The racks that adorned the walls are all gone and in their place are huge black-and-white canvases of a woman asleep, her hair messy and falling over her eyes, as she lies naked on the bed. The pictures are a combination of long shots and close-ups of various parts of her body—a peachy arse, the elegant arc of her neck, swollen lips. She looks sated and relaxed in the close-ups and I suddenly gasp with shock when I realise that the woman is actually me. When I look closer, I can see the faint marks on my bum and realise that Alex must have taken these at some point after our 'vanilla' session.

"I thought we would start over," Alex says softly. His Dom is there in his stance, but the voice is all Alex.

"I like it, sir," I say softly, and honestly I do. It feels different down here now, but I can't quite figure out why…and it is not just a matter of a little redecoration. Maybe it's because I faced my biggest fear and somehow none of that matters anymore; only two people's pleasure of each other does.

Alex comes to stand in front of me and holds out his hand. I take it and let him guide me to the platform in the middle, where he motions me to sit. He sinks down next to me on the comfortable throw and I notice that he has removed his socks and shoes and rolled up the sleeves of his black shirt. The silver tie he was wearing earlier in a loose knot is now unravelled, hanging across the back of his neck and over his chest.

"Olivia, what is your safeword?" Domly Alex is back.

"Daisy," I answer immediately.

"Good. Now I don't care how much you want to please me in here. If you ever feel like you felt the other night, you have to use your safeword. Understand?" I look up into his eyes and see how serious he is. That night definitely broke something in him.

"Yes, sir. I promise."

"And I promise you now that it is my responsibility in here to make sure you never feel like that ever again. I will test your limits, try out new things that maybe aren't in your comfort zone, but I promise never to give you pain again."

"But, sir…" I say, and I can see his eyes narrow at the interruption. "A little pain is fine. I liked the flogger and the crop. The cane not so much."

"Okay, then we can use a traffic light system. Green if things are good, yellow if we need to slow down and back off, and red or daisy if you want to stop. You okay with that?" I nod. "I need to hear you say it, Olivia."

"Yes, sir, I am happy with that."

"Good girl. Now stand up and let me get a proper look at you," Alex says, lying on his back, his hands tucked behind his head and a wolfish smile on his face. I wait in silence as I watch him surveying my body. My skin prickles in anticipation as I hear his breath growing ragged. "Olivia, please go stand in front of the cross," Alex commands, the 'please' a mere formality.

I make my way across to the X-shape that dominates one corner of the room, resisting the urge to reach out and stroke the smooth wood. Instead, I wait as Alex lazily rises and then stalks across to me. Coming to a standstill in front of me, he pauses for a moment as if gathering his thoughts and then brings his lips down on mine with a growl. I expect the kiss to be fierce and intense, yet it is soft and sensual. Without thinking, I find myself winding my arms around Alex's neck, my fingers threading through his hair and tugging the ends as I lose myself. I am only vaguely aware of being backed up until I feel the cool, silky wood behind my back. Reaching behind his head, Alex takes hold of my wrists and gently removes them. Taking each wrist in turn, he kisses the soft skin on the inside before securing it in a wide leather cuff. Once he is satisfied that my arms are comfortable and the cuffs secure, Alex kneels and turns his attention to securing my ankles.

I am completely open, spread out across the cross, and while I feel completely vulnerable, I also feel aroused to the point of pain. I desperately want to rub my thighs together to alleviate the ache that is building in my pussy, but I am denied the friction in this position. A moan erupts out of my mouth as Alex begins to trail kisses across the bare skin above the tops of my stockings. His tongue traces a path over my sensitive skin, punctuated with the odd nip with his teeth at random intervals. I am lost in the sensation when I suddenly feel a stinging sensation across my arse. I yelp and look down at Alex, who is staring at me with hooded eyes and a wicked grin. I can't see a crop or flogger and then I realise he doesn't need one; he simply pulled back the elastic and let it flick backwards onto my skin with a sharp smack. I can feel Alex's cool fingers soothing the sting, and the heat starts to radiate through me.

Slowly Alex stands and takes a moment to look at me. I can see his arousal in his eyes and in the large bulge in his trousers, and I find myself grinning, glad that I am having as much of an effect on him as he is on me. "Please, sir," I say softly, "I'd like to see you, please."

"How can I deny such a sweet request?" Alex responds before quickly stripping off his clothes and tossing them aside. Standing proudly erect in front of me Alex murmurs, "Do you like what you see, Olivia?" I nod my head, words failing me as I lick my lips. "Well, that's enough seeing for a moment," Alex says, and I notice the grey tie from earlier in his hands. Gently, Alex binds my eyes and I am plunged into darkness. "I'll be back in a second," Alex lets me know.

"Okay," I say, my voice hoarse. I hear Alex moving about, a cupboard door being opened and closed, a clinking noise and then suddenly the room is flooded with music. There is a techno beat that seems to bounce off the walls and that seems at odds with the deep voice of the singer. It takes me only a moment to realise that I am listening to German and I quickly recognise that I am listening to Rammstein's 'Du Riechst So Gut'. The music seems to pulse through me and I desperately want to feel Alex's hands on me. I hear him return and sense Alex kneeling down between my legs.

"Okay, Olivia, time to play, baby. I need you to take a deep breath and trust me, okay?"

Oh fuck, what the hell is Alex going to do to me? "I trust you, Alex," I answer before I feel something cold slip between my wet folds. I squirm as he runs it over my clit. "Oh, you are so juicy, baby," I hear him murmur as he swirls the object around my slick entrance. I am becoming needy and my body has started moving of its own accord. "Not here, Olivia," Alex says as I try to push myself down onto the object in Alex's hand. Suddenly the object is gradually pushed into the delicate rosette of my bum and I cry out at the fullness I feel. A moment later a gentle vibration starts up and slowly the pulsing sensation threatens to overwhelm me.

Suddenly Alex is standing in front of me, his hands running across my pliant body. His lips find mine in a fierce kiss that leaves me breathless. I am blind, but it feels like every other sense is on red alert. The buzz in my backside is relentless, distracting me as every now and again Alex snaps one of the elastics on my skin. Underside of my breast...snap. Stomach...snap. Nipple...snap. Each time, the stinging sensation is soothed by Alex's mouth or cool fingers, causing the heat to radiate through my core. Without warning, I hear a snipping sound followed by a sting against my pussy lips as the elastic on my thong is cut. And then Alex's mouth is on me, his tongue teasing my clit as he swirls it around and around.

My need is at a tipping point, and as if sensing this, Alex stands and brings his cock to my entrance. "You ready for me, Olivia? This is going to be hard and fast, baby." I hear the feral tone in Alex's voice and all at once I am desperate to look into his eyes.

"Please, Alex," I plead, "Sir, please, I need to see you."

At once, Alex rips the tie from my eyes whilst simultaneously plunging into me. I am immobile, tied to the cross, and utterly at Alex's mercy as he grabs my arse cheeks and slams into me over and over, all the while his eyes never leaving mine. I can feel my climax building and somehow I know that this is going to be epic. Every nerve in my body seems to be electrified, but it is not until Alex brings his hand down between our bodies and starts rubbing my clit furiously that I explode. I fling my head back and scream out my orgasm as I detonate, my body going supernova under Alex's incessant attention. A hand grips my chin and forces me face to face with Alex. "Open your eyes, Olivia," Alex commands, and I force them open. With a loud growl, Alex comes, his hot seed spilling into me, setting off a chain of orgasms that leave me weak and breathless. The plug in my arse is still vibrating and I just can't take anymore.

"Please, Alex, the plug, too much. Can't take anymore," I gasp out. Instantly the sensation stops and I feel Alex gently tugging it out of me as he kisses me softly. Our bodies are slick with perspiration and I know the only things holding me up at this point are the restraints and my heels, which feel as if they have been ground into the floor.

"Let me get you down, Liv," Alex murmurs as he quickly releases me. Scooping me up, he gently walks me across to the platform and lays me down on the plush throw. Quietly, he rubs my wrists, ankles and feet before cleaning me up with a warm cloth. "That was fucking amazing, Liv," I hear Alex whisper as I try to keep my eyes open. I feel Alex kiss my hair and then I am in his arms again, a blanket wrapped around my body as we head upstairs. I wind my arms around Alex's neck and nestle my head into the crook, completely sated.

*~*~*~*

It is still dark when I wake, feeling uncomfortable and restrained. The glow of the digital clock tells me it is only 1:00 a.m., so I move silently past a sleeping Alex to go to the bathroom. I close the door before flicking on the light, pausing to stare at myself in the mirror. My hair is dishevelled and my lips are swollen from Alex's kisses. I am still in my underwear, so I quickly slip off my stockings and remove my bra and garter.

I stare at my body, which is left with the imprint of the elastics cross-hatching across my skin. My skin is still slightly pink where Alex snapped the elastics and I can see a couple of tiny bruises forming. But there is nothing to mar the ecstasy I felt when I was bound and completely at Alex's mercy. My submission is absolute and I know there is nothing that I wouldn't allow him to do to me. Alex owns me, heart, body and soul.

A small noise startles me and I whip my head around to find Alex leaning against the door frame nonchalantly, his arms crossed as he studies me with a soft smile. "Hey," I say. "Sorry, I didn't mean to wake you."

Alex strides across the room and comes to stand behind me in front of the mirror. "You are so beautiful, Liv," Alex murmurs into my ear as he runs his hands lightly up my arms. Embarrassed, I duck my head to avoid Alex's eyes, but he gently forces my head back up so that I am looking at myself in the mirror. "I will never, ever lie to you, Liv. So you need to believe me when I tell you that I think you are the most beautiful person I have ever met." I am quiet as I try to absorb Alex's words. "You are kind, generous and thoughtful. And your total submission is the most precious gift I have ever received. So yes, to me, you are the most beautiful person I have ever met."

I have no words to respond, so I just smile back at Alex's reflection, a soft expression I have never seen before on my face. "These are very sexy," Alex murmurs, running his deft fingers across the lines covering my breasts, causing me to giggle as he finds a couple of my ticklish spots.

"I need a shower," I say. "Want to join me?"

With a nod, Alex leads me into the shower and spends a couple of moments adjusting the water jets until hot water is pouring over both our bodies. Reaching up onto my tiptoes, I wrap my arms around Alex's neck and pull his lips down onto mine. It feels like we kiss for hours, the steam swirling around us, but before long Alex gently untangles us and grabs my shower gel. Rubbing it between his palms until it has formed a frothy lather, he proceeds to run his hands across my body. When he reaches my shoulders, though, he starts to massage my aching shoulder muscles and I find myself groaning at the sweet pain as he works out the kinks and knots that have developed. When at last I am putty in his hands, he rinses us both down before stepping out the cubicle and grabbing two warm, fluffy towels off the radiator. He wraps one around my shoulders before securing the other around his waist.

We have barely said a word to each other, but it is as if we are speaking a language of our own through touch, looks and sighs. Wrapping his arms around me, Alex pulls me into his embrace. I let out a soft sigh and rest my head on his chest, my arms bound to my sides under the towel. I am dead on my feet and can feel my body swaying slightly as the exhaustion settles over me. A second later, Alex scoops me up and walks me through to the bedroom before laying me down on the bed. With an exquisite tenderness, he dries my body before pulling up the duvet over our spent bodies. Within moments, I am fast asleep.

# CHAPTER SEVENTEEN

I let out a sigh of frustration as I hit yet another dead end in my search for Charles' current book conquest. I thought I had finally tracked down the original to a dealer in the USA, but when I had the paper stock checked it turned out to be a twentieth-century forgery. Damn it. At least I didn't have to travel this time and face the dealer's wrath in person when I informed them that the book that they were hoping to sell for five thousand pounds was worthless.

I glance up at the clock on the wall of the sunroom and decide to call it a day. I have been working from home all week while Charles has been abroad for work, which has made a nice change from having to commute across town to his office in London's Docklands. I make my way into the kitchen to make myself a cup of tea when I hear my phone ring. Not recognising the number, I contemplate letting it go to voicemail, but then I wonder if it could be someone coming back to me on one of my queries, so I pick it up with a business-like 'Hello?'

"Pumpkin?" All it takes is one word and my world seems to start spinning out of control.

I take a deep breath before answering, "Daddy?" And just like that I am thirteen again.

"Oh, pumpkin. I am so glad I have finally tracked your number down."

The memory of how my father had been trying to blackmail Alex flares up in my mind and immediately I feel my body tense up. "What do you want, Dad?" My voice is harsh as I pull myself back from the shock of hearing his voice.

"Oh, sweetheart. I am so worried about you, darling. When I found out what kind of man you are married to, I knew that I had to do something. I have to protect you from that monster." My head is spinning. What the hell?

"He is not a monster, Dad. I love him," I blurt out. I am so angry at his words that my hands have started shaking and I sink down into a chair at the table.

"My girl," he says, his voice laced with concern. "You can't believe his lies. You need to leave him straight away. I am so worried about your safety." I have no idea where this is headed, so I let him continue. "I have a friend that can sort out a quick divorce for you and then, when you get the payoff you are due, you can start afresh and I will be there to help you with anything you need."

In that instant, I see exactly what my father is trying to do. If he can't get the money through Alex, then I am the next target. My voice is as cold as ice as I reply, "You can forget about any money, Dad. I signed a prenup that means I walk away with nothing. And do you really think that showing up after twenty years, I am instantly going to listen to anything you say?" My anger is creeping through my voice. "Yes, Daddy, where exactly have you been while I slogged my guts out to look after Mum, huh? Scamming people in the US, I hear. Well, go crawl back under that rock you have been hiding under. Otherwise I will be getting Alex to turn you in to the Feds. No, actually, I will do it myself!" I am shouting so loud down the phone that I haven't even noticed Alex appear by my side.

"You are just like that fucking whore mother of

yours," I hear my father respond as Alex is removing the phone from my hand.

"James, this is Alex," he says, an icy calm in his voice belying the anger that I can see rippling through Alex's body. "Shut your fucking mouth now and listen very carefully, because I am only going to say this once." Alex pauses briefly before continuing. "If you ever talk to Olivia, come anywhere near her—no, scratch that—even fucking think about her again, I will make sure that you end up in a nice American jail where the inmates will know exactly how you treated your wife and little girl. You understand, you shit?"

There is a brief pause where I guess my dickhead father is agreeing to Alex's demands. "Good, because I am sure the inmates won't tolerate a prick like you. This is the end of this, you hear?" And with that, Alex ends the call and crouches down in front of me, taking my trembling hands in his own sturdy ones.

"Liv, it's okay, baby," Alex soothes, wiping away tears that I didn't even realise were falling.

"I am so angry, Alex," I say. "How dare he?" I stand up quickly and start pacing backwards and forwards as Alex just watches me carefully. "I mean it. He was a crap dad, but there were times when I just wished he would come back into my life. What a joke is that?"

"It's not a joke, Liv," Alex says quietly. "In an ideal world everyone would have an awesome dad in their lives. But you got a raw deal. A shit who couldn't see the gifts he was given and then chose to piss them away. You are better off without him, Liv."

I am so worked up that I just can't seem to stop the rage flowing through me at the unfairness of it all. I sink to the floor as sobs wrack my body. "While I was dealing with my mum's illness, there were times that I would wish he was back to help me…just so I wouldn't be alone. How fucked up is that?"

Alex sinks down and pulls me into his lap, his arms wrapping around my shaking body. Rocking me gently, he whispers into my ear, soft words that wrap around my wounded soul. "Liv, you are not alone. I will always be here. I am not going anywhere, baby. You are mine and I will protect you until the day I die."

We stay like that, on the floor, Alex wrapped around me like a blanket until a buzzing noise brings us both back to the present. Grabbing his phone, Alex quickly scans the message. "Shit," Alex says softly.

"What's up?" I ask.

"That was my mum. She's in a cab, on her way from the airport. She thought she would surprise us."

"Okaayyyy…." I say. Oh shit, I think to myself, as I try to banish the emotions I am feeling regarding my deadbeat father. I attempt to get out of Alex's lap, but he pulls me back into his embrace, placing a soft kiss on my forehead.

"Liv, seriously. I am here for you, okay?" Alex says, looking into my eyes.

"I know," I say softly. "What did I ever do to deserve you?" I ask stroking Alex's cheek lightly. With that, Alex brings his mouth down onto my mine, kissing me gently as he runs his hands through my hair.

"Alex…" I eventually say against his mouth.

"Hmm?" he responds.

"I need to sort my face out before your mum arrives. Otherwise, she will know something is going on, and I don't want to worry her." I pull away from Alex regretfully and he gives me a rueful grin.

He stands and then helps me up in one fluid movement. I give him a quick peck on the cheek before running up the stairs so that I can assess the damage. Once in the bathroom, I splash cold water over my face before vigorously towelling it dry. My eyes are still red-rimmed, but my complexion is no longer pasty. I am just about to dig out some powder when I hear the doorbell go and the muffled sounds of what appears to be an argument. Dropping my powder brush, I quickly hurry onto the landing to see that Sheila has arrived and Alex is standing next to her, his posture tense. I am about to call out to her when she spots me, her body tensing immediately, and I can see the anger rolling off her. For a moment, I wonder if maybe I am projecting my own feelings onto her, but I quickly dismiss this thought; Sheila is hopping mad.

"Both of you, kitchen now!" Sheila spits out, taking off in that direction, everything about her demeanour letting me know that she means business. I glance down at Alex wide-eyed, but he simply shrugs his shoulders, obviously more used to his mother's temper. I skip down the stairs quickly, my heart hammering and a sick feeling in my stomach. This is so not going to be good.

Alex grabs my hand in a reassuring gesture and we make our way in silence to the kitchen, where we find Sheila pacing restlessly. "Sit down," she says, pointing to the breakfast bar, and we both comply immediately. Somehow it feels like I am fifteen again, being told off by my mother, and I have to shake my head to try to dispel the image in my head.

"Righto, so which one of you would like to explain this?" Sheila asks, her tone of voice snippy and hostile as she slips a document in front of us. I blanch as I take in the prenuptial agreement that both Alex and I signed. Even normally cool-as-a-cucumber Alex has visibly paled. Before either of us has a chance to say anything, though, Sheila suddenly fixes me with a stare and asks, "So how long did you know my son before you married him?"

Oh. Fuck. Before my brain can engage, my mouth suddenly blurts out, "Two weeks." 'Oh fuck' is right and I find my hand slapped across my mouth in an unconscious effort to silence myself. I daren't look at Alex, so terrified am I that I have let him down in this crucial moment. But a second later I feel his hand slide across my thigh, giving it a gentle squeeze of support. My mind is whirling, and as Sheila fixes us both with a narrow look, I feel my heart thumping so hard in my chest it feels like it is going to burst at any moment.

I am startled when Alex speaks, his voice low and steady. "Mum, this is nothing to do with you."

"Like hell it isn't," Sheila spits out. "You bring this girl into the family. You had the audacity to stand up in front of our whole community and pledge your love for a stranger. You lied to us, to your father and me, and then you think you can go on merrily sleeping with other people and all that crap because it's okay, it's an arranged marriage and all that nonsense!"

Shame fills me and I can't bear to look at Sheila any longer. I deserve her wrath. I hated lying to her all those months ago and I should have known life was going too well. Something was bound to give.

"Shut up, Mum. You don't know anything, okay?" I can hear the strain in Alex's voice. "And where the hell did you get hold of that anyway?"

"That's not the point, Alex!" she yells, and I can't take it anymore.

"Sheila, please," I interrupt. "None of this is Alex's fault. He was helping me out." I can't stand the idea of him being in trouble with his mum, and if I have to take on the blame and she hates me forever, then so be it.

Sheila whips her head around and looks at me, her gaze positively glacial.

"I, uh..." Oh, shit. This is so hard. I close my eyes and take a deep breath before speaking. "I was at rock bottom and my mother was about to be kicked out of the facility she was in because I couldn't pay the fees." I can feel the tears threatening to fall, the remembered feelings of despair washing over me. "Alex won the bid on a book we were both going after at an auction, and I knew that if I didn't get the book, I would be fired. So..." How the hell do I get around this, I think to myself. "So I explained my situation and Alex took pity on me..." I trail off, not sure how to come out of this without sounding like I have prostituted myself.

Confusion crosses Sheila's face and I can see the cogs in her brain whirring as she pieces things together. "But you didn't have to marry her, Alex," Sheila says softly.

"Didn't I, Mum?" Alex says pointedly as some unspoken communication passes between them. "What about all that Becca stuff, huh? All those hints about how she had come back to work in the family business. How she wasn't married. How we were always suited. Your thoughts on how the estates could function better if they were joined. Blah, blah, blah."

The anger rolling off Alex is now matching his mother's and I just wish the earth would open up and swallow me whole, when suddenly a thought strikes me. "Becca, you mean the Becca?" I ask Alex softly. "You never said…" I trail off as Alex nods stiffly. Realisation dawns and I see that our arrangement had been about saving Alex just as much as me. But I am hardly going to tell Sheila that.

Some of the anger suddenly leaves Sheila and I realise how tired she looks. I mean, she has come all the way from Australia and has just spent the last fifteen minutes yelling at us. Who wouldn't be exhausted? Alex, however, doesn't seem to notice the change because all of a sudden he is on his feet, his arms down by his sides, his hands clenched so hard his knuckles are white.

"Mum, just shut the hell up. And leave Liv alone. She has had to deal with enough shit this afternoon without you barging in and yelling at her like a banshee." Alex is not shouting–far from it, in fact— but his posture and tone of voice are demanding Sheila's attention. I suddenly realise that somehow Alex has managed to manoeuvre me so that his body is shielding mine and I am no longer in Sheila's direct sightline. He is protecting me. My heart swells at this thought, but I am not about to let him take all the flak.

"It's okay, Alex," I say, stepping back out from behind him and slipping my hand into his to let him know that we are in this together. "Your mum has every right to be angry at me." I wish that I knew how to defuse the situation, when a strange look passes over Sheila's face and she suddenly goes pale. In an instant, Alex is by her side guiding her to a stool as the stress of the situation and exhaustion take their toll, murmuring something quietly in her ear. Feeling completely useless, I do the only thing I can think of…make a pot of tea.

It is only minutes before we are all sat back down with a cup of tea each, and I am grateful when Sheila starts to get some of her colour back, but brace myself for the next barrage. When it doesn't come forth, I glance at Alex, but all he does is purse his lips together. Clearly he is as clueless as me.

We are both startled when Sheila speaks again, her voice gentler now. "Oh, Alex, you sook. That stuff about Becca, it was just to rile you up, you idiot."

"What the fuck, Mum?" I gasp at Alex's use of the F-word and I look over as he stares at his mother with a look of pure incredulity.

"Don't you use that word with me, Alexander Edward Davenport!" she snaps. "You refuse to ever bring women to meet us. You never talk about who you are dating. I know for a fact you are not gay. You are thirty-six years old and I don't know if you have ever been in a relationship. I was trying to bait you into saying something, anything. I seriously didn't expect you to go and get married."

Both Alex and I stare at Sheila with mouths open. What the hell? I suddenly see a twinkle in her eye. "Besides, I don't think Becca would probably ever go near you again…not after you left her tied to a tree in the orchard."

I have seen Domly Alex, I have seen passionate Alex, I have seen cold Alex, but I think it is safe to say that I have never seen Alex so thoroughly embarrassed. Yet his cheeks are tinged red through his tan and he is currently beating his head against the countertop.

"You knew about that?" Alex rasps out, unable to look his mother directly in the eye, and I quickly swallow down the giggle that is threatening to escape. This is so not the time to laugh and it comes out as a soft snort instead.

"Yes, Alex. I think most of the town knew about that. Mothers know everything. I thought you would have learnt that by now." I can see Sheila is trying to hold back a laugh herself.

"Fuck!" The word is said so softly and I see Alex tense as it slips out, but I guess Sheila chooses not to hear it and says nothing. Instead, she narrows her eyes at me and I wait to see what is coming next. Yet all she does is watch me. Eventually, though, she speaks up, her words soft. "Do you love my son, Olivia?" I am Olivia rather than Liv, so I know I am not in her good graces, but her tone is even.

"Very much, Sheila. Alex saved me. Literally. He is the most amazing person I have ever met." I feel shaky, but my voice is strong.

A look of approval crosses Sheila's face and then she turns to Alex. "And what about Olivia? Do you love her?"

Alex's expression softens as he looks at me. "Yes, Mum, I love her with all my heart. I knew she was the one for me before I even knew her name." Sheila stares at her son in wonder for a moment, before a smile crosses her face.

"All right then..." Sheila seems to sway a little. "I think I need to have a sleep. Didn't get a wink on the plane."

"Yeah, because you were probably spending sixteen hours planning on how you were going to rip me a new one, Mum?" Alex says snidely.

"Precisely," snaps Sheila, but there is no malice. "Righto, I am going to have a nap and then we are going for some dinner. Alex, can you bring my bags up?" I leave Alex to escort his mum up to the guest suite that, not so long ago, I had been occupying.

I am emotionally exhausted by everything that has just happened, but in a really strange way, I am grateful that Sheila knows the truth. I hate lying full stop, and the deception that I have played a part in has always sat uncomfortably with me. I lay my head down on the cool countertop as I try to collect myself, allowing the silence to soothe me. After a couple of minutes, I realise that Alex has not come downstairs, so I make my way up to the first floor to see if he is in our room. There is no sign of Alex, so I surmise that he is probably with his mum and, not wanting to intrude, I decide to lie down on the bed and wait for him to come down and find me.

*~*~*~*

A soft voice and hand brushing my face wake me from a strange, disjointed dream. I turn on my side to find Alex lying next to me, his expression intent. "Hey," I say softly.

"Hey. How are you doing?" Alex asks, and I can see the concern written across his features.

"I'm okay. Tired. Sorry, I fell asleep. I was just waiting for you to finish up with your mum. What time is it?"

"Six thirty. I have booked us a table at Medlar for some dinner in an hour. Is that okay with you?" I nod my consent and struggle into a sitting position, my body still tense from all the anxiousness earlier.

"Is everything okay between you and your mum?" I ask tentatively. "I am so sorry about blurting that out. Mouth engaged before brain and all that," I joke weakly.

"It's fine, Liv. We talked some more. I am not sure how long it will take for her to get over us lying to her, but mostly we are forgiven. I think it helped that we actually do have feelings for each other. I think she will end up spinning this as some kind of fate thing in her romance-obsessed mind," Alex says reassuringly.

I stretch my arms above my head in an attempt to work out the cricks in my neck and then mutter that I need a shower. I am just stepping out of the warm steam when Alex saunters in naked. I take a moment to let my eyes wander over his delicious body and he smirks back at me, his expression knowing. I barely have a chance to let out a squeak of surprise at what I am feeling, then he is walking me up back into the shower and pushing me against the wall, his mouth on mine in all-consuming kisses. Gently, he uses his knee to push my legs apart and then, with one firm thrust, he is entering me. I can feel my nails digging into Alex's back as I hold on to him desperately. In one swift movement, his hands are suddenly under my thighs, hoisting them around his waist, so that he can sink even deeper into me. I cry out as he finds the right spot buried deep within me and then I find myself biting down onto Alex's shoulder as my orgasm rolls through me. My inner muscles clamp down onto Alex's rock-hard cock and moments later I feel him twitching and spilling into me as he grunts through his own climax. Panting, we both crash back down to earth moments later and I find myself grinning.

"A bit more relaxed?" Alex asks with an insufferable grin and I actually find myself going pink in response. "You look so cute when you blush like that," he continues.

"Pah, grown women shouldn't blush," I say. "And I am certainly not cute."

Alex just smirks at me and starts to wash his body as I rinse off the fact we have just had steamy shower sex.

As I stare into my wardrobe rails ten minutes later, I unconsciously pull on clothes that seem to match my mood. Dark grey tailored trousers combined with a lighter grey jumper and a dark grey scarf. I don't even think of it until Alex follows me in still towelling himself off and raises an eyebrow. I know on the surface I am pretending everything is okay, but all this stuff with my dad, and now Alex's mum, has taken its toll. Truth be told, despite the awesome shower sex, I am just feeling overwhelmed.

"Hey," says Alex quietly, coming to wrap his arms around me. "It's all going to be okay. I promise." I nod as I hug him back hard, nestling into his chest. I glance down at my watch and see we have only about fifteen minutes until we need to leave, so I hurry over to the mirror to finish my makeup in an effort to disguise my pale skin and puffy eyes. I have just finished applying some mascara when Alex emerges dressed in black jeans, black skate shoes and a light blue shirt that moulds to his body, the arms rolled up as always. I offer him a smile and he holds out his arm as he says, "Ready?"

The conversation between the three of us remains light as we walk to the restaurant chattering away about the frustrations over my latest treasure hunt. Sheila has returned to calling me Liv, making me feel utterly relieved and hopeful that I can repair the damage to our relationship. When we have finally slid into a bright green leather booth and settled on what food we want to order, I find myself slowly relaxing. Alex and Sheila are both chatting with the sommelier, going over the recommendations for the meal, when suddenly Alex's phone rings.

Excusing himself, Alex walks away to a private spot and spends a couple of minutes having a very intense conversation with whoever is on the other end. I watch Sheila watching Alex's rigid posture and I am slightly worried when I see him angrily push the phone back into his pocket. By the time Alex returns to the table the tension is rolling off him, and I can see my worry reflected in Sheila's eyes.

I am about to ask Alex if he is okay when he turns to Sheila. "Mum, where did you get our prenup?"

I can see Sheila weighing up her options before replying.

"It arrived via FedEx a few days ago at the house, addressed to me," Sheila says softly. "There wasn't a note attached, and to be honest, I wasn't really thinking about who had sent it once I started reading it." Alex nods and runs his hands through his hair in agitation.

"Would you still have the packet it came in, do you think?" Alex asks. I can sense something is going on and I call Alex on it, needing to know what the hell that phone call was about.

"Probably, back at the house. I would need to call your father to have a dig through the bins," Sheila says, the worry in her voice apparent. "Let me call home." Sheila leaves the table for a short while. While she is gone, I ask Alex what is going on again, but he simply ignores me. He continues to stare down at the table like he is trying to contemplate a solution to world peace or, in this case, who the hell would send a document like that to his mother.

"Okay, Alex," Sheila says sharply, as she slides back into the booth, "you have five seconds to start talking and tell me what the hell is going on. Your dad couldn't find the packet, so in all likelihood, it was chucked when Maria was around earlier in the week, and yesterday was bin day."

"Shit!" exclaims Alex loudly, and I am really starting to wonder if Alex is about to lose it. "I think someone is trying to destroy me—destroy Liv and me, that is. I am not a hundred percent certain and I don't have definitive proof, but things are starting to slot into place."

"Okay…" says Sheila, as she waits for him to continue. "Maybe you should start at the beginning." Oh shit. If Alex is really about to tell his mother about all of this, she is going to want to know why he was being blackmailed. I can see Alex is thinking the same thing, and for a moment I glimpse the insecurities he has buried so deep beneath his usual persona.

"It's okay, Alex," I all but whisper. "I think you need to tell her." I slip my hand into his and give him a reassuring squeeze.

"Oh, Mum…" Alex lets out a deep breath before

he starts his explanation of how my father came into his office to blackmail him. I can see Sheila is desperate to ask a million questions, but she manages to keep quiet and let Alex talk. "There were photos, Mum, and I just knew that I couldn't let them get out. It would damage the Davenport brand and I just couldn't risk all the hard work that you and Dad have put in all these years. If it had just been about me, I could have dealt with it, but there is no way I could let the family get dragged down with me..."

Sheila raises an arched eyebrow. "Photos?" Alex goes red and I can see how exposed he is feeling. "You mean of your...um...kinky fuckery? Isn't that what that *Fifty Shades* lady calls it?" I feel myself going bright red and Alex nearly chokes on the sip of water he has just taken.

"What on earth do you know about *Fifty Shades*, Mum? And kinky fuckery, for that matter?" Alex mutters. This is so not the conversation you want to be having with your mother. I look over at Sheila and I can see the twinkle in her eye. I guess it is not often she manages to ruffle Alex.

"I may be your mother, Alex. But I am not dead. And anyway, where do you think you got it from, huh?" Sheila says with an actual smirk.

"Too much information, Mum. Seriously!" Alex barks out. So far he is has been studiously trying to avoid eye contact with his mother, but he is now looking at her straight on. "How did you know?"

"Oh, Alex," she replies gravely, with a soft sigh. "I already told you...a mother generally knows these things. Plus you started showing an extraordinary interest in knots when you were sixteen and those magazines you kept under your bed were not exactly innocent. Who do you think used to vacuum under that damn thing anyway? And then, of course, there was the whole Becca thing..." I can see Alex just wants to die, but I am relieved at the complete lack of judgment coming across the table.

We are suddenly interrupted by the arrival of our food and for several minutes the conversation is put on hold as we tuck into our meals. My crab raviolo with samphire is delicious; I hadn't realised how hungry I was until I took the first mouthful. When the starters have all been finished, Sheila looks across at Alex and says softly, "Oh, honey. Is this why you left Perth?" Alex nods but stays silent.

"I am going to ask you one question about this, and then you can forget that this conversation ever happened." Sheila pauses briefly before continuing. "Have you ever hurt anyone—I mean, that didn't want it?"

I can see Alex processing her question and taking a deep breath. "No, Mum, everything I have ever done has been entirely consensual." Alex's words are barely above a whisper and I can see it is taking every ounce of self-control not to run out of the restaurant.

"Well, there you go..." Sheila says brightly, as if we haven't been talking about her son's sexual preferences. "Alex, you are every bit the man your father and I brought you up to be. So what if you like it a bit different in the bedroom? As long as you have never brought harm to anyone, then I don't care. You will never 'dishonour' the family name. And you should know us better than to think we would ever think that, son." Sheila looks at me suddenly and I see comprehension dawn, but she holds her tongue as I squirm under her scrutiny until she gives me a discreet wink. Oh my god, this conversation is disturbing on so many levels.

"Okay, so now that is out of the way, where are we at with the whole Liv's dad trying to blackmail you scenario?" I think Alex is just so grateful to be past delving into his whole sexual history that unwittingly he lays open the whole mess that is my family, including my dad's phone call earlier today. "Oh, sweetie. You know your dad is an idiot, don't you?" Sheila says, taking my hand and giving it a sympathetic squeeze. I try to shrug off the horrible weight in my chest that keeps pressing down when I think of how he has treated me, but the tears that just don't seem to want to go away rise to the surface.

In an instant, Alex's arm snakes around my frame and he pulls me against his muscular frame as he soothes me. Just feeling him against me seems to calm me and after a couple of seconds I am feeling much better. Enough to ask about the phone call that started this whole damn conversation.

"The Club," Alex says succinctly. "After I found out about the photos, I contacted the owner, who I have known for a long time. He has been away for the last couple of weeks so has only just been able to review the CCTV footage in the club."

"They have CCTV in there?" I ask, stunned that they would have footage of what went down in there.

Catching on, Alex quickly responds, "Not on the main floors, no, but at the entrance and in some of the corridors. Everyone has to stow their cameras and phones in the locker rooms, so I asked them to check if anyone was seen with a camera phone in the corridors. And lo and behold, the night my picture was taken, there was someone in the corridors with a phone." Alex's expression is dark and I am actually starting to feel a little sorry for whoever is going to be on the receiving end of Alex's wrath. No, scratch that, I want to fucking claw their eyeballs out!

"Who?" I ask, my voice low.

"Sofia." And with one word I am instantly transported back to New Year's and the bitch who ran her nails down Alex's jacket and then proceeded to glare daggers at me all night.

"But why?" I ask and I can see Sheila's raised eyebrows across the table.

Alex nervously looks at me and I know instantly I am not going to like what he has to say. But I try to stamp down any feelings of jealousy that are about to rear their ugly head, particularly in light of how stunning I remember the woman was.

"Sofia and I had a thing for the last couple of years. It was nothing exclusive, mainly just about scratching a mutual itch." Alex sighs and I see him throwing his mother an apologetic glance. "But it was a bit more than what I had had with other women in recent years and I guess Sofia thought it was going to become more significant. About six months ago I ended things with her; she was getting a bit too intense and it wasn't where I wanted things to go. She seemed to take it fine at the time, but now I am wondering whether maybe suddenly getting married so soon after might have riled her up…"

"You think?" I exclaim incredulously. Seriously, for a bloke who is supposed to be able to read the finer nuances of the female psyche, he has just about ignored the elephant in the room. Even Sheila is looking at her son like he has lost the plot. "Is there actually any proof that it was her? I mean, you said my dad said the package he received was anonymous. And we don't have the packaging from the document your mum was sent. Unless we have definitive footage of her taking those photos, there is not much we can do…"

"But the fact that she is trying to mess with me like this, sending stuff to my mum, for heaven sakes, I can't just let it go," Alex says defensively.

"I am not saying let it go, but I think we are going to have to be smart about this. Look, she apparently knows enough about you to know which buttons to push, like sending a copy of our prenup to your mum, but she is obviously resourceful enough to try and find our weaknesses, like my dad." Suddenly, a thought strikes me. "How the hell did someone get a hold of our prenup? Surely that should have been completely confidential?"

"I don't know," responds Alex, and I can see how stressed out this whole thing is making him. We all fall silent for a moment, which is perfect timing, as our main courses suddenly arrive at the table. None of us is particularly hungry, so much of the delicious food gets pushed around the plates. For the most part, Sheila has let the last part of the conversation flow but after a few minutes speaks up.

"Alex, I just want you to know that your father and I love you no matter what. How you live your life is no one else's business but yours. And for the record, however it came to be, I am really glad that you and Liv found each other." Sheila pauses and I can see the emotion in her eyes. I lean across the table and give her hand a squeeze and a smile. "Just be true to who you are. That's all we could ever ask."

By the time the meal is finished, Sheila has caught

us up on all the gossip from back home, and the atmosphere is definitely feeling lighter. I am emotionally exhausted but utterly relieved that all this drama has not caused a rift between Alex and his mum; I know just how precious family is.

# CHAPTER EIGHTEEN

I have had the shittiest day, and to top it off, it feels like I am coming down with something; my limbs ache and I feel hot and shivery at the same time. I don't think I have ever been so grateful to have my front door in my sightline. All I want to do is get out of my sodden clothes and have a cup of tea and a warm bath. Why is it that February weather always has to be so foul?

I have just closed the door and am in the process of hanging up my coat and towelling my hair, cursing the fact that I forgot my umbrella, when there is a short knock at the door. I am so not in the mood for visitors but slap on a smile because, hey, you never know who it might be. Yet when I swing the door open, I seriously wish I hadn't bothered.

Sofia stands on the doorstep, not a hair out of place, looking resplendent in her dark coat and slash of bright red lipstick across her thin mouth. Before I have a chance to say anything, though, she pushes past me into the hall. After you, I think sarcastically to myself.

"Alex isn't here," I say, fixing Sofia with a glare. Right now I seriously wish that Alex wasn't on his business trip to Zurich with his mother. After the impromptu flight to come and tear strips off us, Sheila decided to stay for a week and then head back to Australia via Switzerland to tie up a couple of international deals they had been working on. Cursing the fact that he will not be back until tomorrow, I know I just need to suck it up and deal with Sofia myself.

Sofia narrows her eyes at me, looking me up and down and taking in my bedraggled state. "I know," she hisses, before stalking off in the direction of the kitchen. Damn, I wish that I didn't know that she had been with Alex before because right now jealousy is starting to rear its ugly head, making me even crankier than I was feeling before. I follow in her wake, almost feeling like an intruder in my own house, such is the confidence that she is projecting.

"What do you want, Sofia?" I ask, trying to keep my voice calm and neutral in an effort to not let her know that she is getting to me.

She turns and plants her hands on her hips. "I have come to warn you."

"Warn me?" I ask, wondering where the hell this is going.

"Yes," she spits at me in a viper-like hiss. "Alex is mine. And when your year is up, you will be out on your arse and then Alex will come back to me. Where he belongs."

My mind is spiralling as I take in her words. "Alex broke it off with you, Sofia. I really don't think he has any interest in going back there." I say, the snarkiness I am feeling creeping into my voice.

"You know nothing, Olivia. Your little arrangement that you have going on…that's all it is. He might have pity-fucked you at New Year's, but that is all you will ever be—a wife to keep his family happy. But you will never be enough for him, enough for his tastes." And there she has hit on my weakest spot…my fear that I can't give him what that sadist in him needs. It is as if she senses my inner unease because she continues, her voice harsh. "Because I am. We are yin and yang. Our connection is true to the core. I gave him everything he needed and he loved it." She stresses the words 'everything' and 'loved' and I feel like I have been punched in the gut.

"Yet he still left you, Sofia," I counter harshly, my inner bitch finally making a proper appearance, and I am somewhat gratified when I see her wince slightly.

"Whatever!" she responds, bitterness lacing her words like poison. "It was only ever a matter of time before he came back to me. But you," she says, pointing her finger at me, her blood-red nails talon-like, "you had to go and get mixed up in our business. When my cousin saw your prenup"—gotcha, I think to myself, as the final piece of the puzzle falls into place—"I knew that I just had to bide my time. A year is doable, and then Alex will kick you to the curb and I will finally take my place as the proper Mrs Davenport."

Oh. My. God. This woman is unhinged. Sofia is shrieking at me, garbling about soulmates and yin and yang again, her eyes wild. I am starting to wonder whether I should be trying to make a swift exit when, suddenly, she stills, her eyes growing wide as she stares over my shoulder in the direction of the door. I whip my head around to find Alex filling the doorway, barely suppressed rage rolling off his tall frame.

"Enough, Sofia," he barks, his voice ice-cold. "How dare you come in here and talk to Olivia like this." Funny how Alex always seems to call me Olivia when he slips into Dom mode, I abstractly think to myself with a weird sense of amusement at the situation playing out in front of me. In a couple of strides Alex is at my side, winding his arm around my shivering frame. "You have caused enough trouble with all your stunts and now you have the audacity to come into my home, behaving like this." I notice Sofia shrinking back a little, and even though I know it is not what nice girls do, I feel a nasty sense of relief that she is finally getting some payback for all the crap she has brought into my life.

With a harshness that makes even me wince, Alex continues, "You are going to regret messing with me like this. You knew exactly what the arrangement was when we got together. You wanted more, I didn't, and that was the end. I tried to spare your feelings at the time, Sofia, but the real reason we broke up was because you are a narcissistic bitch. Good for a fuck and a whip, but if you thought I would ever let you near my family and friends, then you were sorely mistaken."

Alex strides forward and grabs Sofia's arm. She emits a low groan as, I guess, the reality of her situation begins to sink in. "Now you are going to get the fuck out of my house," he says as he drags Sofia bodily out of the kitchen and into the hallway, "and out of my life. If you ever come near Olivia again, you will seriously wish that you had never crossed me." By this point Alex is opening the front door and pushing her out, Sofia's previously immaculate hair now dishevelled and tears falling down her face. She tries to apologise, pleading with Alex for forgiveness, but his jaw is set. "And you can let your cousin know that she should expect to be fired," Alex says as a parting shot before slamming the door behind him.

I sink down onto the bottom step in the cold hallway, the adrenaline still coursing through my veins, as I watch Alex lean back onto the door, his eyes closed as he rubs the bridge of his nose. I can see from the stress lines around his eyes just how tired he is, and from the look of his crumpled suit I guess that he came straight from his last meeting.

As the adrenaline begins to leave my system, I am suddenly struck with just how unwell I am feeling. My skin is clammy and beaded with sweat, yet I am shivering. I close my eyes and lean against the bannister as my vision starts to swirl, desperate to keep the nausea at bay. I am just about feeling like I am going to pass out when suddenly I sense Alex in front of me. "Liv, open your eyes," Alex asks gently as his hands smooth my forehead. I crack open my eyes, wincing at the harsh light flooding the hallway. "Jesus, you are burning up," Alex says.

"I don't feel so good," I respond as, weirdly, I am now seeing two of Alex. The next thing I know, I am being carried up the stairs and being deposited on our bed. Everything is kind of hazy as I feel cool hands stripping off my clothes and a cold cloth on my forehead. I hear a low moan and somehow realise that the sound is coming from me.

*~*~*~*

I am aware of the passing of time in an abstract way, mostly by the sound of voices that come and go. My dreams are vivid and at some point I feel like my skin is on fire amidst a hallucination of being trapped in a burning building. I come to briefly to find myself soaking wet under a refreshing shower, Alex supporting my body as we sit under the steady jets of water.

"Alex?" I croak out.

"Oh, baby, I have got you. Your temperature is

too high. We have to get it down, sweetheart." He smoothes back the hair off my face and I curl myself into his body, my head nestling into Alex's neck. Strong arms encircle me and the murmur of gentle words sends me back into the darkness.

*~*~*~*

I wake to see weak sunshine filtering through the bedroom window and for the first time in what feels like days my mind is clear. My throat is parched, though, and I find myself reaching for a glass of water that I see on the side, only to find a large hand already there and handing it to me. My eyes meet Alex's and their normally slate colour is clouded with darkness and exhaustion.

Alex helps me into a sitting position, packing the pillows around me, and finally, I can take a sip of the cold water he offers. "What happened?" I ask, struggling to put together the pieces of why I am lying here, feeling like I have done ten rounds with Mike Tyson.

Sitting on the edge of the bed next to me, Alex smoothes a stray hair off my face. "You have had the flu, Liv. A rather nasty bout. I wasn't sure if your temperature was ever going to break. Scared the shit out of me, actually." Alex pushes a hand through his hair distractedly and scowls. "Thought I was going to have to get you to the hospital a couple of times."

"The shower..." I say as vague memories flicker through my mind.

"That was last night. Your temperature finally broke about two o'clock this morning." Alex's voice catches and I can see the strain written all over his face. He doesn't look like he has slept for days.

"I am so sorry," I whisper, feeling dreadful that I have put him through this.

"Oh, baby, none of this is your fault. Just one of those things. I am just so relieved you are back in the land of the living." With that, he plants a gentle kiss on my forehead. "Do you want a cup of tea?" he asks, knowing me well. I nod and he disappears through the door.

I lie back and try to piece together the last things that I remember. Images, like a silent show reel, flick through my mind. "Sofia," I gasp out as I finally remember returning home and then being subjected to her rant.

"It's okay, Liv. I dealt with her," Alex says reassuringly as he walks back into the room, holding a steaming cup of tea. I take the cup gratefully, blowing on the top and feeling the warmth of the steam in my face.

"How long was I out?" I ask, before taking a sip.

"Three days," Alex replies, climbing up next to me on the bed. He proceeds to talk me back through what happened, how he finished up his meeting early and thought he would surprise me, and how he walked through the front door just as Sofia and I moved through to the kitchen. He heard all the crazy things she had been saying and then stepped in. Slowly everything falls into place.

"Her cousin? How the hell did she get hold of our prenup?" I ask, still hazy on that point.

"I helped her cousin get a job at the firm of solicitors I use about a year ago. Nothing major, just asked my guy there if they had any openings after Sofia had been upset because her cousin, who had just qualified, was struggling to find a job. Needless to say, after this, she is no longer working there. I spoke to Michael as soon as I could after Sofia let slip to you about the contract, so she is now facing disciplinary action. What she did was beyond unprofessional, and Sofia was a shit for putting her cousin in that position." I take Alex's hand and squeeze it gently.

"You look shattered, Alex. You need to sleep." My cup is empty and I am feeling so tired again. Alex is dressed only in a pair of loose pyjama bottoms, so I pull him towards me, guiding us so that we are both lying down. I caress his cheek with my fingers. "Thanks for looking after me," I say with a soft smile. "I should bottle you." Alex looks at me quizzically. "You know, period cramps...death...the flu. You are always here looking after me, making me feel better."

Alex gives a smirk at my weak attempt at a joke and pulls me into his body. He tangles his legs in mine and rests my head under his chin, before pulling up the duvet to cover us both. Within moments, I hear his breath start to even out as sleep claims him and I can't help but think about how much I love this man who is always there for me, no matter what happens.

# CHAPTER NINETEEN

It has been two weeks since I woke up from my battle with the flu. Two weeks that Alex has played nursemaid to me, insisting that I needed time to rest and recuperate. But now I am bored shitless. Don't get me wrong, the first week was bliss; I slept, I ate and I generally forced myself to try to relax. Hours were spent on the sofa alternating among dozing, reading and watching films whilst Alex sat sentinel, tapping away incessantly on his laptop. But now I am coming up to the end of the second week of bed rest and I am slowly going insane. I have never spent this much time just doing nothing; my body is antsy, my brain itching for some more stimulation than lame TV or sappy romance novels. And to top it off, I am horny as hell.

Last night—after quite a bit of persuasion, I might add—I managed to get Alex to make love to me. Up until then, the most Alex would do is hold me as if I were fragile porcelain; one wrong move and I might break. It was intense, yet gentle, and when we came together, the sparks that washed over me were heavenly. But now I need more. My body is yearning for a hard fuck and the kind or orgasm that comes only when I give Alex my complete submission in the playroom.

When we are in the bedroom there is always the knowledge that I retain my control, yet when I offer myself down in the playroom, I do it with the knowledge that Alex can do whatever he likes with me. I am not sure why the distinction between the two spaces exists and I can only think that Alex works hard to not dominate me in our bedroom yet is happy to in the playroom. All I know is right now I want Alex to take the kid gloves off and fuck my brains out.

I have also spent a lot of the time these past two weeks thinking about Alex and his grand proclamation that he is a sexual sadist. For some reason, this really bothers me and it is something I am determined to get to the bottom of. I can understand his desire to dominate. He comes from a family of people who are incredibly strong-minded, and the more I have come to know Sheila, the more I can see how she has brought up all of her children to take control and get what they want. There is certainly not a pushover amongst them.

My mind flicks back to the words that Alex said to me when I asked if caning me had helped him:

'For a few minutes, I felt centred again, calm and collected like it normally would make me feel, but when you started crying for real, there was none of the excitement, none of the arousal I would usually feel. Instead, I just felt hollow and empty, and terrified that you would hate me.'

If Alex were truly a sadist, then he would have enjoyed my pain, and the crying should have excited him, not caused him to stop. He has told me that he enjoyed spanking and whipping his subs but that he only ever did it with subs who wanted that level of pain, masochists who would get their own gratification from having it inflicted upon them. A win-win situation. If I break it down in my mind, then everyone got what they desired; there was no humiliation and both parties got to enjoy their kink. For me, that doesn't exactly fit with my definition of a sadist.

All I can think of is that in Alex's training under the Doms he told me about, he got this idea in his head that he liked spanking women and, ergo, that made him a sadist. And that brings me full circle back to this whole intimacy thing. A thought slams into me with the force of a train and I know, deep down, that right at the heart of the matter is Becca.

I think about how he told me that they were best friends. Best friends who fell in love and then finally took that momentous decision to sleep together. I recall how he used the words 'romantic' and 'gentle', and even though he had made a throwaway comment about it, I firmly believe that he was in love with her. Putting aside all the other kinky business, essentially Becca broke Alex's heart. With that comes the realisation that Alex's need to put intimacy and love aside stems from the fact that, in admitting who he really is, he lost the first girl he ever loved as well as his best friend. This makes Alex's reaction to his mother's prompts about Becca returning back home even more understandable. The sting of first love's betrayal is bound to cut the deepest and I honestly don't think he has ever gotten over it.

I feel so sad for Alex in this moment that I find myself wiping away a tear that has formed. A cold feeling has seeped into my bones, so I pull a soft throw off the back of the large wing-back chair that I am curled up in and drape it over me. The house is quiet, as Alex is currently out at a meeting, so I return to my inner musings.

The Alex I have come to know and love is certainly a dominant person and I guess that I have allowed him to take that place in my life from day one because it was what I needed. He offered me the opportunity to give up the strangling control that I needed to have on my life the day that he gave me his outrageous proposal. I was so sick of having to always be the one taking care of things that it was almost a relief when he suggested we get married. If I am honest with myself now, as much as I needed the help with my financial situation, I think what really persuaded me was the trust I felt in Alex's presence and his insistence on taking care of me during the year we would be together. For so long I had been the one making all the decisions, especially where it came to my mother, that for someone else to take on that stress was sheer liberation.

The sound of the front door slamming shakes me out of my reverie. I don't immediately make a move to get up and go down. My head feels ready to explode after mulling everything over and I know that I am going to have to talk to Alex about my conclusions. Maybe if I can get him to work through some of this Becca stuff, then he can get some closure and maybe a little insight into himself.

Suddenly footsteps pound up the staircase and Alex comes rushing into the little nook on the landing that I have claimed as a reading spot. I catch sight of his face and gasp when I take in the look on his face. He looks angry—downright furious, actually.

"What the fuck, Liv!" he exclaims, his voice livid. "How could you be so stupid?"

I reel back as if I have been slapped. What the hell? I try to stay calm as I reply, "What are you talking about, Alex?"

Suddenly I see a piece of paper in Alex's hand. What on earth could it contain that could make Alex flip out like this? I wrack my brain, but nothing makes sense. "How can I take care of you and protect you if you don't help yourself?" Alex seethes.

"You are not making any sense, Alex. Please, just tell me what the matter is." I am struggling to maintain my calm in the face of Alex's anger. He has never spoken to me like this and I can feel my body trembling.

"You never got your flu jab. When I think how sick you were, it kills me, Liv. And to find out you could have prevented it…" Alex trails off, handing me a piece of paper. I scan it quickly and see that it is a standard letter from my GP practice. Suddenly I remember receiving the letter the day that my father called and Sheila arrived to tear a strip off us. In everything that happened, I guess I must have put the letter to one side and forgotten about it.

My voice is icy as I respond, "I received that letter the day my dad called to talk to me for the first time in twenty years and your mother verbally attacked me, making me feel like the shittiest person on earth. I am so sorry for not foreseeing that I was going to get ill and rushing out to get my jab, but with everything that happened, it kind of slipped my mind." At the sarcasm in my voice I see Alex's brows shoot upward. I have certainly never talked to him like this before, but then again I have never had reason to.

The fight seems to slip out of Alex's posture as he kneels down in front of me, pulling my hands into his. When I look into his eyes, I am shocked to see them glistening. "Fuck, Liv," Alex says, his voice hoarse with unshed tears. "I just don't know what I would do without you. I love you so much and…and watching you when you were so ill, it just made me realise how much a part of my life you have become. I just couldn't stand it if anything happened to you."

"Oh, Alex," I sigh. "You can't get mad at me for the what-ifs. I have no plans to go anywhere." I reach up and run my hands through Alex's hair, taking note that some of the strain is finally leaving his eyes. I run my thumb across his cheek, stroking his smooth skin, in what I hope is a soothing motion. But instead a burn ignites in his gaze and his eyes become hooded with lust, sending sparks through my gut.

Before I even have a chance to respond, Alex is picking me up and flinging me over his shoulder. "What the fuck, Alex?" I squeak as he strides down the stairs with purpose. Only moments later we are descending the stairs to the playroom, where Alex deposits me rather ungracefully on the platform in the middle of the room. I turn over to look up with trepidation, trying to gauge Alex's mood, but his countenance is blank.

"I want you naked, now, Olivia." Alex barks out his command, and I can feel the muscles in my pelvis tightening with anticipation. I do as he says without thought, stripping off my yoga pants and long T-shirt quickly and then going one step further and taking up my submissive position, kneeling on my haunches, legs spread on the soft fabric of the throw, my arms resting on my thighs with palms up and my face downwards.

I watch from under my lashes as Alex unbuttons his cuffs, rolling them up his arms with deft fingers, before kicking off his shoes and removing his socks. He sits down on the edge of the platform, his thighs spread before he instructs me to come lie across him. I shiver with anticipation as I drape myself across him, locking my fingers together as he has taught me. We have done this once before, a playful spanking session, which had shown me how much pleasure Alex was capable of metering out, but I am sensing something a bit darker today. Maybe it was the fact that he was angry at me or that I was sarcastic in my response, but I get the feeling that this is going to be a bit different. Alex shifts me slightly so that my head is resting on his firm thigh, turned away from him while my bum hangs over his other, my toes barely touching the floor. I can feel his muscles rippling under me and my heart begins to thump. I feel nervous and when Alex touches my back I almost jump out of my skin. I let out a small gasp of surprise, waiting for what is about to come next, but instead of the slap I am expecting, Alex runs his fingers along my spine before burying his hand in my hair. He twists it around his fingers and then gently pulls my head back so that I can just about see his face from my odd angle.

I expect to see anger, but instead all I see is an eerie calm, which is actually more frightening. "You have a smart mouth, Olivia," Alex says, his voice low and stern. "Sarcasm is the lowest form of wit, you know. And I certainly don't expect to hear it coming from you." I watch Alex earnestly, wondering what my punishment is going to be. I am really hoping he is going to tell me because the waiting is causing a whole list of potential ideas to run through my mind, and really, I have no idea what he is going to do.

"And as for your health, I expect you to take every precaution to see that you don't fall ill." I bristle at this statement, indignation coursing through me. While I am fine with him punishing me for my sarcasm, disciplining me for a perceived disobedience seems very unfair.

"Please, sir, may I speak?" My voice is barely a whisper. I have never questioned Alex when we have been in this room and I have no idea how he is going to respond to me now. His eyes narrow on me, but he gives me a brief nod. I pick my words carefully. "Sir, I am happy to accept punishment for my sarcasm, but please, don't chastise me for something that was a genuine oversight during some very trying circumstances." I do my best to keep the tremble out of my voice, but my body is shaking so much now that it is impossible to keep still, despite the rigid hold that Alex is maintaining on my head and the firm palm that is holding my pelvis down.

"In all the time I have been with you, I have never willingly disobeyed you. You once said to me that you had no wish to dominate me outside of this room, yet I freely allow you to direct our lives. I offer up my submission to you on a daily basis, ceding to your demands freely by loving you with all that I am, and not once have I ever given you cause to believe that I would willingly do myself harm." I am horrified when I feel a tear slip down my face. "So please accept my apology for not taking better care of myself. It will not happen again." I let out a shaky breath and slide my eyes away from Alex's, unwilling to watch whatever emotions they contain. For a split second, I consider using my safeword, but somehow I realise that this is a test of our relationship and Alex's actions now could potentially make or break us, so I wait.

It feels like forever before I sense any change in Alex, but in reality it is probably only about a minute before I feel the hand at the nape of my neck relax slightly. "Three smacks for your sarcasm," Alex says, his voice gravelly. I wait for him to continue, and when he doesn't, I let out the breath that I have been holding and nod slightly to indicate my understanding. A moment later, Alex's hand connects with the soft cheek of my arse and I yelp at the stinging sensation that spreads across my buttock. Before I have a chance to focus on the burn that has started to spread to my pelvis, another painful slap lands on my other butt cheek. I brace myself for the third, and when it lands directly over my sex, I cry out loudly. My body has responded to the aphrodisiac of this pain and I can feel how wet I have become. It would appear that Alex is aware of this too as he runs a finger through my wet folds before bringing the finger back to his lips and sucking on it. "Delicious," he murmurs. "Now I think we should do something about this smart mouth of yours." In a gentle motion, Alex tips me off his lap and onto the floor. I immediately scramble back into my submissive position, doing my best to ignore the pain of my heels digging into the sensitive flesh of my behind. I glance up to find Alex towering above me, unbuckling his trousers. In one fluid motion he pulls them down, along with his boxers, and tosses them into a corner of the room. His cock is erect and swollen, the veins bulging along his rigid length, and I can see the end glistening in the light.

"Hands behind your back, Olivia. Lock your fingers together and kneel up. Stay very still because I am going to fuck your mouth until I come. You understand?" I nod my assent and Alex moves closer to me. I open my mouth to take him inside, but he surprises me by running his cock over my lips, spreading his pre-cum over them until they are slick with his moisture. Then he guides himself into my mouth slowly. I run my tongue over his smooth, velvety skin, enjoying the feel of him, but all the while taking care not to move my head. I feel Alex threading his fingers through my hair, anchoring them on my head so that he can control my movements. I start sucking on his engorged cock, hollowing out my cheeks and allowing him to go as deep as he can until I feel him touching the back of my throat.

For a moment I panic, my gag reflex kicking in as my brain tells me that I am not going to get enough oxygen. Immediately Alex stills. "Breathe through your nose, Olivia," Alex instructs. His voice immediately calms me and I do as I am told until the fear has completely vanished. My body relaxes and I feel a sense of peace run through me as I surrender to Alex.

Now that I am calm, Alex picks up the pace, fucking my mouth with long, hard thrusts, each one driving further and further into my throat. Arousal pools in my pussy as I feel Alex swell even more on my tongue. Moments later I feel him twitching, his orgasm not far off, and then he is coming, great hot spurts that slide down my throat. When he finally stills, I hear him panting, and the fingers loosen on my hair though they still stay in place. I feel him softening and then he is slipping from my mouth, leaving me feeling suddenly bereft.

"Fuck, Olivia. You kill me," Alex says hoarsely, and I look up at him from underneath my lashes shyly, wondering what is coming next. I know I have no reason to feel shy—I am a grown woman, for heaven's sakes—but even so his reaction always slays me. I have remained completely still, my hands still linked together and my knees complaining about the hard floor. Alex holds his hand out to me and I unlink my fingers so that I can place my hand in his. He helps me to my feet, which are unsteady as pins and needles course through my calves and ankles, and then guides me across to the cross.

I listen quietly as he instructs me how he wants me to stand facing the cross before he straps me up in the restraints. His eyes are hooded as he works silently, and I desperately try to read his body language, wondering if I am in for more punishment or if he is going to make me come. He steps away and disappears from my sightline, the opening and shutting of drawers the only clues to his whereabouts. The next thing I know is that he is standing directly behind me, his breath tickling my neck.

"Just so you know, Olivia," Alex says darkly, "I am going to take you…over and over. You are mine to do with as I wish. And today I am going to own you…here," he says, pushing a finger into my mouth. "And here," he continues, removing the finger from my mouth before thrusting it into my pussy. "And finally, here." He trails the finger coated in my juices around my clit, before pushing it deep into my arse. I let out a gasp, tensing slightly, when it filters through exactly what Alex has planned for me. "Relax, Olivia. I'll make sure you are ready. If it is too much, though, you can always use your safeword." My mind is in overdrive, desire coursing through my veins, and all I can do is nod my acknowledgement.

I feel Alex's erection digging into my back as cool hands snake around and cup my breasts. He merely holds them for a few moments, as if weighing them in the palms of his hands, before his fingers start caressing my nipples. The buds harden into stiff peaks, and when he pulls on one hard, I cry out, electricity shooting through my core. Suddenly Alex's hands leave my breast and I groan at the lack of stimulation. And then Alex's hands are back. I glance down to see him holding out a couple of ornate butterflies in his hand and my mind swirls at the purpose. Before I can say anything, Alex is tugging at one nipple and then affixing a butterfly to it. Seconds later he has repeated the process on my other nipple and instantly I understand. The pain is sweet and, at once, my pussy feels like it has a direct line to my nipples. Even the lightest of brushes stokes the arousal building inside of me.

Alex's hands run across my back and across my hips until one sneaks around to cup my mound, the palm of his hand pressing down on my aching sex. Without a thought, I find myself grinding against Alex's palm, trying to get some friction to alleviate that pulsing sensation that seems to match my frenetic heartbeat. "Stay still," Alex growls, landing a stinging slap on my backside. The pain immediately morphs into a dull pleasure that seeps into me. A moment later, Alex is pushing two fingers into me with one hand and playing with my clit with the other. The sensations, combined with the continual throb of my nipples, are too much and, suddenly, I am coming hard and fast.

They say there is no more erotic instrument than the mind, and at that moment I immediately understand where that came from. Alex begins to whisper dirty thoughts into my ear and the images that they conjure make me writhe against his hard body. At some point, Alex had dispensed of his shirt and now I can feel the sweat beading on the bare skin of his abdomen. The swirling of my clit never ceases, and then Alex is entering me from behind, my greedy pussy welcoming the hard steel of Alex's cock. He rocks into me slowly and I groan as I feel his lips sucking on my neck. I am helpless, constrained by my bindings and completely open to Alex as he starts to fuck me harder.

I have completely lost my ability to think coherently and instead I am a mass of sensations and swirling colours as Alex pushes me closer and closer to the brink. I welcome the orgasm that shatters me, taking me higher than I have ever flown. Lights dance behind my closed eyelids as I feel Alex slip out of me. Suddenly I feel Alex nudging my arse, his cock slick with my juices. The pressure builds as, very slowly, he pushes himself in, inch by inch. I gasp as pain floods through me, but Alex's voice in my ear soothes my nerves. Suddenly he is pulling off the nipple clamps and my body fills with endorphins, distracting me from the unwelcome intrusion in my backside. Using the opportunity, Alex thrusts himself deeper until I feel his pelvis against my bum cheeks. He stills for a moment to allow my body to stretch and get used to him but never lets up in his incessant swirling of my clit.

The burn in my backside slowing fades and, instead, the fullness that I feel starts to overwhelm me. Slowly Alex begins to move, the catalyst that sparks a different kind of orgasm in me. I groan as he picks up speed, the pressure building until I explode, pulsing around Alex and setting off his own climax. I am still flying high when I feel Alex bite down on my neck as he thrusts his fingers deep into my wet pussy, as he remains buried in my arse. I vaguely hear Alex call out my name as the final waves of my own climax move through me.

I am panting hard when I finally become vaguely aware of my body. I am utterly spent, yet when Alex gently removes himself out of me, I cry out at the loss. Within moments, Alex has untied me and is carrying me across to the platform where he lays me down. I am still struggling to drag myself out of my orgasm-induced fog as I lie there limp and sated, when Alex returns with a warm washcloth. He cleans me up with tender strokes whilst the tingles and shivers finally fade from my body. A moment later, he is pulling me into his arms and wrapping us both in a warm blanket.

We lie there in silence, bodies thrumming as Alex softly runs his fingers across my sensitive skin. After a while, our heartbeats return to their normal pace and I start to wonder if Alex has actually fallen asleep, when I suddenly feel him nuzzling my ear.

"I am so sorry, Liv," Alex says and I know in an instant that he is not apologising for what he has just done to me—not that I would want him to because it was amazing. No, he is apologising for getting angry at me and wanting to punish me for something I had no control over. I realise that it has probably cost him a lot to make this admission, so I snuggle into his chest.

"Alex, it's okay," I murmur sleepily, gently stroking his bare skin. Moments later I hear Alex's breathing even out and I let myself slide into the darkness.

# CHAPTER TWENTY

At some point during the night Alex must have carried me upstairs because I wake to find myself snuggled under the duvet of our bed. The dim light shining from behind the curtains and the sound of rain beating against the window herald another dull and gloomy February morning. My muscles ache from the night's activities and my head is pounding from the lack of food and hydration. I swing my legs out of bed and go to stand, but stumble when the head rush I experience makes me feel dizzy. I am just sinking back down onto the mattress when Alex walks in with a tray and a look of concern on his face.

"Argh, I think I overdid it last night," I say, dropping my head into my hands. Alex quickly puts the tray down and comes to my side, smoothing back the hair off my face.

"You okay, Liv?" he asks.

"Just a headache," I respond, trying to reassure him. "I just need to eat."

"Then it's a good thing I made you breakfast," Alex says with a grin. I climb back so that my back is resting on the headboard, pulling up the duvet to keep me warm while Alex settles a tray piled high with toast, Vegemite for him and strawberry jam for me, along with giant mugs of tea and coffee between us. We eat for a while in silence, both lost in our thoughts. Part of me wants to bring up the whole Becca thing, but honestly, I have no idea how to start that conversation.

My toast has been eaten and my tea drunk and I am slowly feeling the life come back into my body.

My head is still pounding, though, and I know it is down to the tension in my neck. I roll my shoulders and move my head from side to side, trying to loosen my muscles, but nothing seems to work. A moment later, Alex is placing the tray on the floor and sliding in behind me. He slowly begins to work at the muscles in my shoulders in long, even strokes, teasing out the knots with sure fingers. Eventually, the vice-like sensation on my neck starts to ease and, along with it, my headache. Slowly his fingers work their way upwards in firm, soothing strokes that start a tingling sensation in the base of my spine. Finally, Alex tangles his fingers in my hair, tugging my head back gently so that my neck is exposed.

Slowly Alex starts to kiss my neck, his lips caressing my skin as they move. At one point, he stops and plants the gentlest of kisses on a particular area. It smarts a bit, which confuses me until Alex says, "Sorry, baby. I bit you rather hard last night." Ah, that explains it. The memories of last night flood through my mind and all at once I am completely turned on, my arousal making me wet between my thighs. I subconsciously rub my legs together trying to ease the ache that has suddenly begun.

One of Alex's hands comes around to stroke my breast while the other dips between my wet folds. A finger finds my clit, teasing it with a languid swirling motion while occasionally pinching it, and I find myself leaning back into Alex's chest, allowing the sensations to take over. It takes only a couple of minutes for the pressure to build up, the tingles and sparks to develop into a raging inferno, until I come, gasping in Alex's arms.

A moment later, Alex is sliding out from behind

me and coming around to settle between my legs. With one thrust he is entering me, my back arching as my pelvis tilts to take him even deeper. I look into Alex's eyes as he stares down on me. I see lust, arousal, but most of all, love shining down on me. He takes his time, moving his hips slowly, stoking the burn deep inside. He brings his mouth down to mine, covering my body with his own while entwining his fingers in mine, and I lose myself as his tongue mirrors the movements of his cock. The burn intensifies and it takes only a couple more thrusts for me to come apart under Alex. Seconds later he follows me, spilling his seed deep inside.

Slowly we both come down from our climaxes, legs and arms entangled, making me unsure where my body ends and his begins. We are breathing deeply, and when he lifts his head up I can't help but smile at the look of pleasure on Alex's face. I do that to him, I think to myself. Just little old me.

A short time later we are relaxing in the bath and I have finally steeled myself to open the proverbial can of worms. I am lying back against Alex's chest and I take a deep breath. "What's up, Liv?" Alex asks, sensing my unease.

"Can I ask you a question, Alex?" I say nervously.

"You can always ask me anything, Liv," Alex responds.

"You...you know when you and Becca had sex for the first time?" I feel Alex stiffen at the mention of her name. "And you said it kind of left you cold?" I stumble slightly as a deathly quiet falls across the bathroom. I can hear Alex's heart thumping in his chest, a loud drumming that echoes my own nervousness.

"Okay, where are you going with this, Liv?" Alex asks, his voice low with mixed emotions.

"Sorry, I am not explaining myself properly. Just hear me out, okay?" I feel him nod. "Do you think you didn't feel the spark, the connection, because it wasn't there? Or maybe because you were both just young and inexperienced and had overblown expectations of what it should have been like?"

I can feel Alex absorbing my words behind me, his frame tense. But he says nothing, so I continue. "I mean, we all have these expectations of what sex should be like. We watch movies, read the magazines and stuff, and I guess we are doing it in our heads a long time before we actually get down to it." I pause for a moment, to gather my thoughts, before continuing, "So I guess what I am asking is, do you think that you felt the way you did because you thought you should feel a certain way and then didn't, or because you felt nothing at all?"

"I don't get why you are asking me this stuff, Liv," Alex says, and I can hear the pain in his voice.

I push off Alex and turn around so that I am facing him. "Just hear me out, okay? Let me tell you what I think went on..." I trail off, looking Alex squarely in the eye and wait until he gives me the briefest of nods to let me know it is okay to continue.

"You were a horny teenager, probably got hold of some pornos and magazines somehow. Saw things in there that turned you on, bondage and stuff..." I feel my cheeks heating up. After everything that has gone on between us I can't believe I can still feel embarrassed around Alex. "Probably jerked off a lot to those fantasies. But then when it came down to your first time, if it was anything like mine, it was probably a lot of fumbling around, doing your best to be careful and not hurt the girl who was also your best friend. And ultimately, it was probably over before it even really began…" I raise my eyebrow at Alex and I see a grimace cross his face, confirming my thoughts.

"So you had sex a few more times, and while it was probably nice enough, it didn't elicit the kind of feelings you had when you watched the pornos. Then came the final straw. You tried to get Becca involved in one of your fantasies, but given how inexperienced she was, she probably didn't understand where you were coming from and so—justifiably, I might add—freaked out on you. She called you names, broke it off with you, making you feel ashamed but also breaking your heart in the process." I look at Alex, who has actually paled whilst I have been talking, and I feel terrible that I am exposing such a raw wound. But to be honest, this has been festering for a long time, and if he doesn't deal with it now, it will haunt him forever.

"You are not a sadist, Alex. Somewhere along the line you convinced yourself that you couldn't do intimacy because you liked spanking women and you got yourself all messed up because, basically, you never healed from your broken heart." I lean forward and place my palm on Alex's cheek. "You have shown me over and over that you can do intimacy, you even seem to like a bit of 'vanilla', and you seem to be doing okay—hopefully more than just okay—with the kind of kink we have been indulging in."

Alex is watching me, frozen still as if one movement could set off an explosion. "If you really were the sadist you think you are, then you wouldn't have stopped caning me when I started crying. You would have enjoyed it, revelled in it even. But you didn't. It was almost as if it hurt you worse than me." I drop my hand and sit back.

"You need to let go of these preconceived notions about yourself, Alex. Yeah, you might enjoy doling out a little bit of pain and dominance, but you don't have to put yourself in a box and label it. Life is a journey that we need to travel down to find out who we really are. You don't come out of the womb fully actualised any more than you stay the same person you are your whole life. We evolve, we change, and it is time you accepted that you are not the monster you think you are." I stop, wondering if I have stepped over the line.

Alex is completely silent and I sit there, watching him and hoping that I haven't somehow pushed him away. I go to touch him, but he flinches away from me and I feel the sting of rejection. Without a word, Alex hauls himself out of the tub, grabbing a towel and stalking out of the room.

I stay in the bath long after the water cools and it is only when my teeth start chattering that I climb out of the tub. I dress slowly, determined to give Alex some time to think. Eventually, though, I head downstairs, going from room to room and coming up empty. I am certain that I didn't hear the front door, which means Alex is down in the playroom. Part of me wants to go down there and make sure that he is okay, but the other half is telling me to wait until he is ready to face me on his own terms.

The hours pass slowly and I do my best to keep myself occupied. It's a Saturday, so I can't even distract myself with work. Eventually, though, the sky starts to darken and I decide enough is enough. I approach the door to the basement with caution, my ears straining to hear any discernible sounds. But there are none, so I make my way down the stairs. I am not trying to be quiet, yet the carpet seems to swallow up my footsteps.

The majority of the room is in shadow when I step into it, the only illumination provided by a couple of side lamps. My heart breaks when I see Alex lying on his back on the platform, an arm casually flung across his eyes. I pad over to the platform and sink down onto my knees beside it. "Hey," I murmur, wondering whether Alex has fallen asleep.

"Hey you," Alex responds quietly, moving his arm but not opening his eyes.

"Are you okay, Alex?" I ask, worried about him. He seems calm enough, but I wonder whether this is a prelude to a storm.

"How is it that you managed to see through me?" Alex asks. "How were you able to look into my soul and see the things that I have never even acknowledged for myself?" His voice cracks, and my heart aches for him.

"I think—and I know this sounds trite—that we have a connection. I have felt it since the day we met. Despite the situation, your dominance and all my other worries, the moment I was with you I felt calm. I trusted you. If I believed in that kind of thing, I would almost say that we were old souls that found our way back to each other." I honestly don't know where this has all come from, but the words have just kind of spewed out.

Alex finally opens his eyes but doesn't look across at me. I reach over and slide my hand into his. "It has been bugging me for a while, this whole sadist thing, because it was totally at odds with what I knew about you. And the more and more I thought about it and the things you told me, well, I guess I started drawing my own conclusions. I didn't want to upset you, Alex. Far from it, in fact. I only brought it up because last night we got into a position where your perceptions of who you are could have hurt me—not physically but emotionally. And I figured if you didn't start to face this, well, who knows what that would mean down the line?"

"You were right, you know," Alex says softly. "About all of it. I had never thought about it in that way. Actually, I never let myself think about it full stop. But I think you hit the nail on the head. I have been down here for hours just trying to sort through everything in my mind, going round and round in circles, and I just keep coming back to what you said about me defining who I am, sticking a label on myself so that I could use it as a shield. An excuse for not letting anyone in." Alex lets out a sigh and I can see that he is okay.

"You know," he continues, "you are the first person that I have let in. What you said about soulmates, I think you are on to something there." I look at him in surprise, not sure how he is going to respond to that little outburst. "The first time I saw you, there was this pull, like a magnet. I knew I wanted—no, needed—you in my life. It wasn't sexual because you seemed so innocent and there was no way I was going to allow myself to bring you into that part of my life. It was just that I wanted to be part of your life, anyway that you would let me. I was prepared to be any person you needed me to be, do anything you required."

His words tickle something in my subconscious and suddenly I find a broad smile stretching across my face. Who would have thought it? "So you're a Twilight fan then?" I say. Alex looks at me, startled, with a faint blush rising on his cheeks.

"Kayla made me!" he stutters out.

"Yeah, yeah," I laugh.

"Seriously, she made me sit down and watch the whole lot of them in a marathon on my last trip back to Perth." I hear the disgust in his voice and it makes me smirk.

"Yeah sure, like you would have sat through five films just because your niece made you." I smirk at him. "Man, I love those movies," I say with a giggle. Alex pulls me up onto the platform and over his body so that I am now sitting in his lap.

"But seriously, Liv. I heard what you said last night. About your submission. Don't think I haven't noticed how you offer it up to me, even in the smallest ways. It is the sweetest gift you could ever give me and I don't take that lightly." Alex runs a thumb down my cheek, stroking it gently. "You have captured my heart and I can't imagine a future without you in it."

"We really did this the wrong way round, didn't we?" I say with a laugh. Alex looks at me quizzically. "Well, we got married, then we fell in love. We never even had a first date."

Alex grins at me. "That does sound crazy when you put it that way."

"What, more crazy than getting married only two weeks after meeting you?" I retort and Alex just grins.

Alex gently brings his mouth down onto mine and

I sink into his kiss. Without a doubt, Alex Davenport is the best thing that has ever happened to me. He owns me mind, body and soul. Which should terrify the life out of me, but instead makes me feel cherished and loved. And I guess the secret is that I own his; together we are the halves that make us whole.

# EPILOGUE

It is a year since Liv became his wife and he has been determined to do something special for their anniversary to celebrate. At long last, he is going to take her on a first date. It has taken some planning, but finally he has put together something he thought she would love.

The last year of his life has been full of light. She is the antithesis to the darkness that he had held on to in his soul. She showed him how to become the man he was destined to be and for that he is eternally grateful. She even encouraged him to meet up with Becca to find some peace.

He had always wondered if the way things happened had hurt Becca as much as it had him. When they finally met again, on a trip back home with Liv, he finally managed to get some closure with her assurances that his behaviour hadn't actually scarred her for life. It seems silly now, looking back, to have held on to the angst for so long, but the mind fuck he had given himself over the supposed expectations of others meant he had trapped himself in a cycle of loathing and self-pity.

Alex shakes his head, dispelling thoughts of everyone but Liv. He checks his watch and sees that he still has half an hour before he is due to pick Liv up. This morning he had been in their walk-in wardrobe, trying to find a tie, when he spotted the gorgeous dress Liv had worn on their wedding day. It had been so simple yet classically elegant and perfect for her. When he had found out she had shunned the dresses costing thousands of dollars and picked a simple chain store dress for a couple hundred dollars, he had known that he had a keeper; for too long he had been surrounded by women just wanting him for his money and status. He had pulled the dress out, and when he asked if she would wear it, her eyes had shone. She had simply nodded, tugging on her bottom lip with her teeth in a way that always makes him horny.

He pats his jacket pocket, making sure that it is still there, despite checking it only five minutes ago. He is a little nervous about offering his gift to Liv, though he has no doubt that she won't turn him down. But it took him ages to find the right collar for her and he hopes that she will love it as much as he does. The collar is actually a long chain made of platinum with a small loop in the end. The other end of the chain is fed through the loop and then a beautiful heart-shaped lock is clipped on the end to stop the necklace from coming undone. It is a discreet version of a slave collar, not that he wants Liv as his slave, but since she already has his ring he wanted to offer something more personal as her Dom. Tiny diamonds and sapphires sparkle on the chain and the lock matches. Overall he is rather proud of his choice.

He can't wait any longer and steps into the car. The journey from his office is short, and soon he is pulling up in front of his own front door. He picks up the posy of hot-pink gerbera, Liv's favourite, tied up with ribbon and then makes his way up the steps. He rings the bell and hears Liv's heels clicking on the tile floor of the entrance hall. She opens the door with a shy smile that blows him away. "Happy anniversary, Liv," he says, moving to kiss her on the cheek. "You look stunning."

And she does. She has filled out the dress slightly since their wedding day, making her curvaceous and seriously sexy. He spots the top of her nude stockings as she reaches up to unhook her coat, forcing him to take a deep breath and temper his arousal. His plans for this evening are too important for him to lose it now and jump her like a horny teenager. He helps her into her long black coat, discreetly inhaling her scent as he lifts her hair out the collar. She pulls on a soft scarf, winding it around her neck to protect her from the frigid November air.

A moment later they are stepping out into the snow, his arm around her waist as he guides her across a couple of slippery patches of ice. "Slightly different weather from the last time I wore this," Liv laughs, and he finds himself smiling widely back at this beautiful woman who has captured his heart. He may be her husband and her Dom, but she owns him mind, body and soul.

# ABOUT THE AUTHOR

Bibi is a former marketing executive and mum to a gorgeous little girl currently residing just north of London. She recently spent a year living it up on the beaches of Western Australia and her hobbies include consuming copious amounts of coffee and chocolate, building cardboard castles and creating stories in her head.

Inspired from a young age, her love for literature started with Enid Blyton and her Secret Seven. Since then a voracious appetite for books has brought her a world full of heroes, love, murder, betrayal and the odd vampire thrown in for good cause.

Having long admired those brave enough to put pen to paper, or in this modern age of computing, keyboard to screen, she has finally started telling the sexy stories that she has been keeping locked up in her head all this time.

Visit **www.bibipaterson.com** for more information.

## OTHER BOOKS BY BIBI PATERSON

**Thirty Days series**
Set in London and Brighton, Thirty Days is an erotic romance series that gives you a very steamy love affair between a hot guy and an unsure heroine, baked goods and some rather unexpected twists and turns along the way.

**Santa's Saucy Shorts**
Santa's Saucy Shorts are a series of short, erotic Christmas stories around 5,500 words.

Made in the USA
Columbia, SC
23 November 2017